A small town in Georgia. A family with a past. A trilogy packed with sensual secrets and private scandals!

Meet Savannah McBride. Thirteen years ago her actions scandalized the whole town. And she's been paying for it ever since. Now she's ready to live a little. But is she about to make the same mistake twice?

Savannah, Tara and Emily— the McBride Women. They've come home to put the past to rest. Little do they suspect what the future has in store for them!

SEDUCING SAVANNAH—
January 1998
TEMPTING TARA—
March 1998
ENTICING EMILY—
May 1998

Dear Reader,

Large Southern families are a favorite theme in my books—probably because I come from a rather large one myself. And the McBride family, with their secrets and scandals, their legacies and legends, is very close to my heart. Savannah, Tara and Emily McBride, cousins raised as closely as sisters, all have to find a way to deal with their family's infamous history—as well as their own indiscretions—before they can pursue their dreams and find romance along the way.

While developing the concept for this miniseries, I came across another theme I'd always been curious about—exploring the way the labels we are given in childhood remain with us as adults. Savannah, "the pretty one," labeled a flirt and a party girl, is still dealing with an overdeveloped aversion to gossip. Tara, "the smart one," the one everyone thought most likely to succeed, finds herself facing failure for the first time in her life. And Emily, "the homebody," has been so busy taking care of everybody that she's neglected herself. Finally there is Lucas—Emily's brother—labeled a murderer by the residents of the small town where he grew up. The more I get to know the McBrides better, I'm thinking that Lucas has a very special story to tell....

As a lifelong reader who has found many hours of entertainment in books, I have been truly blessed to be able to pursue a career doing what I love to do—telling stories. And so I'll begin. *Once upon a time in a small Southern town...*

Happy reading,

Gina Wilkins

Gina Wilkins

SEDUCING SAVANNAH

Harlequin Books

TORONTO • NEW YORK • LONDON
AMSTERDAM • PARIS • SYDNEY • HAMBURG
STOCKHOLM • ATHENS • TOKYO • MILAN
MADRID • WARSAW • BUDAPEST • AUCKLAND

For Brenda Chin, my editor,
in recognition of her talent, her professionalism,
her genuine appreciation for this genre, and—
most of all—her patience!

ISBN 0-373-25768-6

SEDUCING SAVANNAH

This edition published by arrangement with Harlequin Books S.A.

Printed in U.S.A.

Prologue

"ARE WE REALLY sure this is such a good idea?"

Kneeling beside a freshly dug hole in the spring-damp, rich Georgia dirt, Savannah McBride looked up at her cousins as she asked the question. Inside the hole rested a mud-encrusted cypress chest that had once belonged to their grandfather, Josiah McBride.

Fifteen years earlier the cousins had filled the chest with personal treasures and buried it in this spot in the woods with the solemn promise to dig up their "time capsule" on Savannah's thirtieth birthday. They were still several weeks shy of that occasion, but they'd impulsively decided to excavate the chest today to take their minds off the reason they were together—the funeral of Savannah's uncle, Josiah McBride Jr.

Now Savannah was having second thoughts about revisiting the past. She winced as she thought of that childish letter, filled with grandiose plans that were so completely different from the way her life had actually turned out.

"Maybe we should wait," twenty-eight-year-old Tara said after a moment. "It has been only fifteen years. Time capsule contents are much more interesting after more time has passed, don't you think?"

Emily McBride, the youngest at twenty-six, firmly shook her head. "We've already trekked out here and dug it up," she said. "We might as well open it."

It was Emily's father who had been buried that morning, after a long, miserable illness through which she had unselfishly taken care of him. And it had been Emily who'd talked Savannah and Tara into changing into jeans and sneakers and following the old path into the woods behind Emily's house to this huge oak tree where they'd spent so many childhood hours, munching candy bars and sharing secrets.

"Besides," Emily added, "wouldn't you rather be doing this than hanging around in the house with all those other people?"

That clinched it, as far as Savannah was concerned. She'd rather wrestle an alligator than go back to that house full of chattering townspeople and cold green-bean casseroles, where she was constantly aware of the surreptitious glances slanted her way, the avid murmurs that stopped as soon as she approached, the carefully veiled comments that let her know the old scandals hadn't been forgotten by the residents of tiny Honoria, Georgia.

"Your children aren't with you today?" several had politely inquired, even knowing that Savannah rarely brought her twins to this place where they would be eagerly studied for family resemblances, where they were likely to overhear gossip that would only hurt them.

Go back to the house? Not until she absolutely had to, Savannah thought flatly.

"Okay, cousins. Let's see what's in here," she said, dragging the old chest out of the hole.

Mud had seeped through the cracks and seams of the wooden trunk. Her hands protected by gardening gloves, Savannah plunged in and pulled out the filthy contents, while her cousins leaned close to watch.

The three shoe-box-sized plastic containers protected within the bags still looked almost new. Each box had a name written on the lid in faded permanent marker. Savannah picked up the first one. "Tara," she said, reading the childishly formed letters.

Looking uncertain, Tara reached out to take the box from Savannah. She held it as gingerly as if she'd packed it with explosives all those years ago, Savannah thought with wry amusement.

"Where's mine?" Emily asked.

Savannah handed her the appropriate container and Emily moved away, staring at the box with a mixture of anticipation and fear.

The final container in the chest had Savannah's name written on it with a flourish of curlicues and squiggles. She hesitated a moment before picking it up. Waves of memories flooded her mind, whirling, crashing, almost overwhelming her.

The first ten years of her life had been almost fairytale perfect. "Daddy's little princess," she'd been. She could almost see him now, coming home from a hard day's work with sweat on his brow and a gift for her in his shirt pocket—gum, candy, a pretty ribbon, an inexpensive bracelet. It didn't matter. She'd loved them all, because she'd adored him. How he'd spoiled her, telling her she was pretty, she was smart, she was talented, that she could be and do anything she wanted.

And then he'd died.

Savannah's mother had continued to spoil her, though in her own odd, almost prosaic way. Ernestine, who'd grown up on the wrong side of the social tracks, had urged her pretty, popular daughter to be everything—head cheerleader, homecoming queen, sought-after date.

Savannah winced in response to memories that were almost too painful to contemplate.

"Savannah?" Emily prodded. "Aren't you going to open your box?"

Savannah wanted to refuse. Wanted to shove the box and the trunk right back into that hole and cover them with dirt, to stomp it down and pretend she could do the same with the memories. But then she looked up at Emily and saw the rather lost expression in her younger cousin's wide blue eyes, and Savannah's heart twisted in sympathy.

"Yes," Savannah said gently. "I'm going to open it."

By unspoken agreement, they moved apart. Savannah had packed the contents in layers of newspaper. *The Honoria Gazette.* She was tempted to look through the old pages, but her attention was drawn, instead, to the objects they had protected.

There was a small tiara, studded with rhinestones that spelled out Junior Miss Honoria. A miniature royal-blue-and-white pom-pom to represent her envied position as head junior-high cheerleader. A program from a school play, in which Savannah had played the lead. A dried-up corsage. A photograph enclosed in a clear plastic sleeve—herself as freshman prom queen, wearing a formfitting, shimmering blue gown and standing beside her date, Vince Hankins, captain of the football team. Every girl in town had wanted to date him. Savannah had felt like the luckiest girl in the world when he'd turned his frequently fickle attentions her way.

She stared blankly at that photograph, remembering....

Remembering the time he'd hit her for smiling at another boy. He'd left a bruise on her cheek. She'd told everyone she'd fallen.

Remembering the way he'd made her cry by telling her that she would be nobody if he dumped her. That the girls who envied her and emulated her would turn on her if he declared her "uncool." She'd believed him. Rightly so, it had later turned out.

Remembering the night of her sixteenth birthday, when he'd made her prove her love for him in the back seat of his father's Cadillac. She'd cried all night, then had to wear extra makeup to school the next day to hide the evidence. That was the day he'd given her his class ring to wear. The envious looks she'd gotten from the other girls had almost made her forget the humiliation of the night before.

She'd been an idiot. Blind. Gullible. Shallow. Needy. And when she'd become more trouble than she was worth to Vince—when she had become pregnant less than six months after that first clumsy bout of experimentation—he'd dropped her like a hot coal. And so had all those "friends" who'd formerly surrounded her.

She'd been so young when she'd packed this box. Fifteen. Shallow and materialistic, obsessed with her looks, with possessions and popularity. And yet she'd been so eager and hopeful, so certain that everything she wanted would come to her in time. Vince Hankins had stolen that optimism from her along with her innocence.

She forced her thoughts back to the earlier memories, those precious times with her father. She'd been so blissful then. Even when she'd buried this box, she'd been happy, thriving on the attention she'd received, naively unaware of how quickly envy could turn ugly.

She shouldn't have let Vince take her happy memories along with everything else, she realized with a renewed surge of anger.

Thoughtfully, she looked at her cousins, wondering if the memories their treasures had evoked were any more pleasant than her own. Tara's expression was unreadable, but it wasn't hard to tell that she wasn't happy. Emily looked stricken, her face pale as she stared down at something she held in her hand. Savannah didn't know which of her cousins needed comforting most. She hardly felt in a position to help either of them.

She looked down at the box in her hand, at the unopened letter lying among the other mementos. And she knew she couldn't open it, at least not just then.

First, she had to look long and hard at what her life had become. And then, she had to decide if she wanted it to remain that way.

1

HE WAS WATCHING her again.

Savannah glanced across the outdoor dance floor toward the man who leaned against a palm tree on the far side. Tiny white lights strung overhead combined with flickering candlelight from the tables surrounding the dance floor to cast intriguing shadows on his handsome face, increasing the air of mystery surrounding him. She thought of him tonight as a pirate, an illusion enhanced by their Caribbean surroundings, by his loose black shirt and fitted black slacks, by the longish dark hair that tumbled carelessly over his forehead.

He fascinated her.

She took a sip of her champagne and told herself that the bubbles must be going to her head. Just because the man was sinfully gorgeous, just because he seemed to be staring at her every time she'd spotted him, there was no reason for her to get carried away by fantasy.

And yet a tiny voice inside her kept asking, Why *not* get carried away? This vacation on Serendipity Island was the last reckless adventure of her twenties. A chance to remember what it was like to be young, free, daring...and totally without responsibility for the first time in thirteen years.

An orchestra played from a raised platform at one end of the dance floor, filling the perfect, tropical night with sultry music. Couples swayed and twirled, talking softly, merging in the shadows, looking so happy and cozy that Savannah felt a twinge of envy.

That was something else she'd never had, she mused. Romance. True intimacy.

Was it too late?

A shiver of awareness coursed down her spine, causing her to look again in the direction of the man in black. He was making his way toward her, a look of determination on his face that caused equal reactions of excitement and wariness within her.

He strode through the maze of tiny tables and ornate little chairs with a natural grace and fluidity that made her mouth go dry. His eyes locked with hers from several yards away, letting her know that he'd had enough of just watching her. He was making his move.

And that challenging little voice inside her said, *Go for it, Savannah.*

He could have stepped straight out of a foolish, romantic fantasy, she found herself thinking as she watched him walk toward her table. His dark, layered hair looked windblown and touchable. Angelic dimples combined with the devil's own smile. Six feet of lean, tanned, firm body. Thick-lashed dark eyes that could cajole a woman into doing something incredibly unwise.

He held out his hand to her, the gesture both inviting and a bit arrogant. *A pirate's move,* she thought. And his voice was as smooth as old Southern sippin' whiskey when he said, "Dance with me."

The orchestra began to play a new number, one that Savannah recognized immediately. "That Old Black Magic."

Was this magic? Or just her long-starved romantic

imagination being fed by the island, by the music, by this man's dangerously beautiful smile?

She placed her hand in his.

And almost gulped when his fingers closed around hers—strong, warm, alive.

Undeniably real.

He led her to the dance floor, then turned to take her in his arms. Their gazes locked when he pulled her close to him, the jolt of physical awareness as apparent in his expression as she knew it must be in hers. A sense of wonder filled her as he studied her face for a moment, seeming to memorize every feature, before he began to move.

His shoulder was broad and strong beneath the soft silk of his shirt. Savannah could feel his warmth through the fabric. Well-defined muscles shifted beneath her fingertips. She very nearly shivered in response.

She hadn't danced in ages. Longer than she could remember. Yet she danced with this enigmatic stranger as if they'd had years of practice, as if they knew by instinct when to turn, when to sway, when to move apart, when to come back together.

What was happening between them?

"What's your name?" he asked her, never taking his gaze from her face.

"Savannah." She didn't add a last name; details seemed unnecessary in a fantasy.

He rested his cheek lightly against her hair, bringing them slightly closer together.

His voice was a low rumble in her ear. "Kit."

"Excuse me?"

"Kit," he repeated. "My name."

Kit. A suitably piratical name for this man in black, she thought with a private smile.

The orchestra was playing "Bewitched" now. How could they possibly know exactly what Savannah was feeling?

She was vividly aware of the heat of Kit's right hand at the small of her back. The thin fabric of her filmy black dress provided little barrier between his warm palm and her suddenly-sensitized skin. His left hand was still closed around her right, his hold firm, almost possessive. As if he had no intention of releasing her anytime soon.

She didn't want him to release her. Being this close to him felt much too good. She could go on like this for hours.

Kit smiled down at her when the orchestra broke into a new, swingier number, "Cheek to Cheek," from the Fred Astaire/Ginger Rogers movie *Top Hat.*

"Ready for this one, Ginger?" Kit asked, demonstrating that he, too, knew the song.

"I'm game if you are, Fred," she replied with a smile.

He promptly swung her away from him, then pulled her more tightly against him. "'Heaven. I'm in heaven,'" he crooned in a better-than-adequate imitation of Astaire.

And Savannah knew she was dangerously close to falling for him. How could he possibly know that she was a pushover when it came to old movies and old songs?

Kit ended the dance by dipping Savannah back over his arm in a dramatic move worthy of the big screen. She clung to him, laughing and breathless, for once uncaring of what anyone around them was saying about her. Who cared? She would never see these people again. Tonight she was having more fun than she'd had in a very long time, and she intended to savor every moment of this magical evening.

Kit didn't immediately release her, even after the music stopped. Savannah's smile faded as their eyes met, locked. She wasn't aware of the other dancers, of the orchestra members moving off the stage for a short break, of anything except Kit's body pressed close to hers, his mouth hovering inches above her own.

She swallowed hard as her pulse began to race.

Careful, Savannah, she heard the voice of common sense warn her. *This isn't real. It isn't safe.*

But that other voice, the reckless one that had encouraged her to dance with Kit in the first place, said, "Forget safe. This is incredible."

Very slowly, Kit steadied her, then stepped a few inches away from her. "Have a drink with me?" he asked, his tone again somewhere between a request and a command.

She had to clear her throat before she could speak coherently. "Yes."

He nodded with the air of a man who was accustomed to having his invitations accepted.

Who was he? Savannah wondered as they made their way back to the table. A high-powered business executive, perhaps? An entertainer? He was certainly good-looking enough. While he looked vaguely familiar, Savannah couldn't say for certain that she'd ever seen him before.

As he held her chair for her in an old-fashioned gesture that only further entranced her, she decided she didn't care about details. Tonight he was her pirate—her fantasy—and she wouldn't let reality intrude.

Kit murmured an order to a server, who returned almost immediately carrying glasses of champagne. Kit sent Savannah a rakish smile as he lifted his glass. "Here's to dancing beneath the stars," he said.

She almost sighed. What a memory this evening would make when she returned to the hectic grind of her real life, she thought dreamily. "To fantasies," she murmured.

Kit's dark eyes glinted in the candlelight. He raised his glass to his lips. Savannah sipped her own drink, reveling in the heady effervescence. The expensive champagne tasted the way she felt tonight. Frivolous. Bubbly.

Intoxicating.

Kit kept his gaze on her face. "Savannah."

Even her name sounded exotic when he said it. "Yes?"

He shook his head slightly. "Nothing. I just like saying your name."

Oh, he was good. She could almost feel herself being seduced, right there. She knew she'd have to be careful not to carry the fantasy too far—but she wasn't quite ready to call an end to it just yet.

The musicians returned to the stage and launched smoothly into the opening notes of "As Time Goes By."

"I love this music," Savannah murmured, feeling as if she'd drifted back to an earlier, more romantic era.

Kit promptly stood. "Then let's not waste it," he said, and held out his hand.

CHRISTOPHER PACE, known to his friends as Kit, couldn't stop staring at the woman in his arms. He was having a difficult time deciding what it was about her that had enthralled him since the first time he'd seen her, sitting alone on a beach at this resort that seemed filled with couples.

She really was beautiful, he mused. Her honey-blond hair had fallen to below her shoulders when he'd seen her before, and was now twisted into a loose knot at the top of her head that looked as though it would take only a brush of his hand to make it come tumbling down. She wasn't a girl—closer to thirty than twenty, he guessed—but he liked the way her mature curves had filled her tastefully revealing bathing suit, and were now displayed so enticingly by her floating black dress.

Her face was unlined, complexion close to perfect, and her eyes were a clear, bright blue that seemed very much in keeping with the tropical setting. Her accent was Southern—slow, soft, musical, making him fantasize about warm, lazy days and long, sultry nights.

Kit had known a lot of beautiful women. He'd discovered at an early age that the beauty on the outside didn't always represent what lay beneath. He'd learned to value a quick mind, a sharp wit and a kind nature much more than a pretty face and figure. And, from his first impression, Savannah seemed to have all of that.

But the attractive packaging didn't hurt, either, he was honest enough to admit to himself.

The orchestra was playing "Misty" now. Kit rested his cheek lightly against Savannah's hair and enjoyed the feeling of her moving so sinuously against him. The scent she wore was very light, faintly floral, just enough to tickle his nose and tempt him to bury his face in her throat for a more extensive sampling.

He had to hand it to his pal, Rafe Dancer, the owner of this island resort. Rafe provided his guests with the best of everything. This new, spectacular dance floor was ringed with fragrant flowers and swaying palms, close enough to the beach for the steady rush of waves to provide an exotic undercurrent to the music being played by the small but excellent orchestra.

Kit moved with Savannah into a tight turn that caused her breasts to brush against his chest. He winced and put a bit more distance between them.

He was definitely aroused by this woman, Kit realized, amazed at how quickly, and how powerfully the attraction had struck. He'd known from the moment he'd first seen her that he had to meet her, even though he'd come on this impulsive vacation to be alone. He hadn't been looking for Savannah—but he was very glad that he'd found her.

He had no intention of letting her slip away until he'd had a chance to explore more fully the heady and extraordinary feelings she evoked in him.

KIT'S STEPS took on a new intricacy as they grew increasingly comfortable dancing together. Savannah concentrated on following him, which wasn't particularly difficult since he was so very good.

"You're better at this than I am," she admitted ruefully, smiling up at him.

His answering grin was a flash of dimples and a gleam of white teeth. "Just hold on tight," he said suggestively. "We've got all night to practice."

And then he spun her into several tight turns that made her cling to him and laugh softly. With only a few words of encouragement and the guiding support of his hands, Kit soon had Savannah feeling like Ginger Rogers. She'd never felt freer or happier in her life.

This was a memory she would treasure forever.

The musicians took another short break, during which Savannah had another glass of champagne with Kit. He sat very close to her this time, and rested his hand on the back of her chair, so that his fingertips brushed her nape when she moved.

Each time he touched her, she felt a quiver of awareness race down her spine. Though the ocean breeze that fanned her exposed skin was pleasantly cool, she was growing increasingly warm, the heat sizzling deep inside her.

It felt good, she decided. A bit frightening, but good.

She was going to have to be very careful with this man, she thought as they returned to the dance floor.

After a few upbeat numbers that stretched Savannah's newfound dance talent to the limits, the orchestra slid into a slower, more leisurely song. Kit pulled Savannah close, sliding both his arms around her waist so that hers had nowhere to go except around his neck. Taking advantage of the opportunity to catch her breath, she rested her cheek against his silk-covered shoulder, barely swaying with him in time to the music.

"Mmm," she murmured in pleasure. "I like this number."

Kit turned, and she followed effortlessly. "'I Have Dreamed,'" he whispered against her ear. "It's one of my parents' favorites. They love to dance."

His voice softened when he spoke of his parents, and Savannah found herself even more drawn to him, if that was possible. She wondered a bit wistfully if *her* parents had ever danced in the moonlight. She couldn't imagine her straitlaced and repressed mother indulging in such a frivolously romantic evening.

Savannah decided not to think of her mother just then.

The few other couples remaining on the dance floor were very quiet, moving dreamily in rhythm to the romantic music. Without pausing between numbers, the musicians began a song Savannah recognized immediately.

"Star Dust," she murmured.

Kit nodded against her hair. "One of *my* favorites."

A man who loved old songs, looked like a movie idol, and danced like Fred Astaire. Was it any wonder Savannah was all but melting in his arms? She couldn't have imagined a more perfect fantasy.

Inevitably, it was time for the idyll to end. "Midnight," Kit said with a glance at his watch as the musicians left the stage and the waiters began to clear the tables. The other couples were already drifting back to their cozy cabins.

Savannah swallowed a sigh. The time had flown by so quickly, she thought with a touch of regret. But now it had to end.

She brushed a stray strand of hair away from her face and smiled at Kit. "It's been a lovely evening," she said. "Thank you for making it so special."

"I'll walk you to your room," he offered immediately.

She bit her lip. She didn't want this almost perfect interlude to end with an awkward encounter at her door. If Kit was expecting to spend the rest of the night dancing between her sheets, she would have to disappoint him. As attractive as he was, she simply couldn't tumble into bed with a handsome stranger she'd known for only one evening.

No matter how spectacular she sensed it would be.

He seemed to read her expression. "I don't expect you to invite me in," he promised a bit gruffly. "I'd just like to see you safely to your door."

Though Savannah had felt perfectly safe ever since she'd arrived at this exclusive resort, she didn't bother to argue. She merely nodded, deciding to trust Kit to continue to be the gentleman he'd been so far.

He took her right hand, slipped it beneath his left elbow and held it there in a courtly manner befitting the tone of their magical evening. And then he began to walk down the comfortably lighted path in the direction of the guest cabins, setting a casual pace that Savannah had no trouble matching in her strappy heels.

The evening air was cool against her flushed skin. The light breeze was heavy with exotic fragrances, reminding her again of how far she was from home. How free she was to enjoy this romantic interlude.

She was so glad now that she'd dared to be irresponsible and impulsive and self-indulgent for the first time in almost longer than she could remember. She *needed* this vacation.

"Will I see you tomorrow?" Kit asked when they reached the door of her cottage.

She moistened her lips, wondering how she should answer. Maybe it wasn't wise, but she wanted very badly to spend more time with Kit. The reckless part of her urged her to take advantage of every moment she could have with him. Who knew when—if ever—she would have an opportunity like this again?

"I'd like that," she said, fighting uncharacteristic shyness when she met his eyes.

"Have breakfast with me."

Again, it wasn't a command, yet not quite a request.

"Please," he added with one of those dangerous smiles.

She bit her lower lip. She wasn't looking for a holiday romance. And anything more serious was out of the question. She would bet her modest little diamond-stud earrings that she and Kit had absolutely nothing in common beyond a fondness for old songs and dancing in the moonlight.

Still, what could another few hours together hurt, as long as she didn't let things go too far? A few laughs, some light conversation, a little harmless flirting...could that really be so bad?

She could almost hear her mother responding to the mental question. *Don't be a fool, Savannah Jane. You, more than anyone, know what kind of trouble you can get in if you don't behave yourself.*

In response to that familiar, carping voice, Savannah lifted her chin and said almost defiantly, "All right. What time would you like to meet?"

Kit's smile deepened. "Eight-thirty?" he suggested. "I'll stop by for you."

She nodded. "Fine. Eight-thirty."

"Maybe we could go down to the beach after breakfast," he added, pressing his advantage.

She murmured something noncommittal, deciding to take the next day as it came.

Moving slowly, as if to keep from startling her, Kit leaned closer. "Goodnight, Savannah," he murmured, his warm breath brushing her lips. "Sleep well."

"Good night," she whispered, her breath caught in her throat.

He kissed her lightly at first, apparently intending to keep it brief and friendly. But something changed almost immediately after their lips met. What had begun as a tentative, rather innocuous caress was soon transformed into a deep, thorough, intimate embrace.

It was the first time in her life that a kiss made Savannah feel as though she'd been struck by lightning. The powerful charge coursed through her from her lips to her toes, which curled automatically in her high heeled sandals. It sizzled beneath her skin, igniting the heat that had been building inside her since their first dance. Desire exploded inside her.

By the time Kit lifted his head and backed away, Savannah was incapable of speech. She could only stare at him, stunned by what had just happened between them. Kit's dark eyes looked rather glazed, and his breathing wasn't entirely steady. She wasn't the only one who'd been affected by the kiss, she thought dazedly.

He hadn't even touched her except with his lips, she realized, and yet her entire body tingled as though he'd run his hands over every inch of her. How had he *done* that?

She couldn't handle this, she thought as panic coursed through her. She wasn't experienced enough to keep her responses to this man under control. It would be too easy to get in over her head, and she refused to let another charming, seductive, overconfident male shake the hard-earned self-confidence she'd spent thirteen years building.

As if he'd read her mind—and seen her doubts—Kit spoke quickly. "Tomorrow morning. Eight-thirty. I'll pick you up."

He was gone before she could find her voice to argue with him. As he faded into the shadows of the long walkway that circled the resort compound, she thought she heard him humming "Star Dust."

Savannah closed herself into her tidy little cottage and then leaned back weakly against the door.

"Oh, my," she murmured, fanning her burning face with her hand. "What an evening."

And she would be seeing him again tomorrow.

BY THE TIME Kit was to stop by for her the next morning, Savannah had convinced herself that she'd simply overreacted the evening before. She'd let the champagne, the stars, the music and the dancing go to her head, she decided.

No man could be as incredible as Kit had seemed to be last night. Dashing gentleman pirates were only fantasies, and she would do well to keep that in mind in the light of day.

She'd dressed casually today, wearing denim shorts and a red-and-white-striped T-shirt over her royal blue swimsuit. Barely-there sandals on her feet. Her hair pulled back into a flirty, twisted ponytail. Looking into the mirror, she saw echoes of the girl she'd been fifteen years ago, when she and her cousins had buried that silly time capsule. Back when she'd looked forward to each new day and the adventures it would bring.

She lifted her chin and nodded in approval as that old, slightly reckless feeling surged again inside her for the first time in so very long. She was on a tropical island, about to meet an attractive and entertaining man. She was going to enjoy every minute of her time with him, darn it. She could do that without causing a disaster, right?

"Right," she firmly told her doubtful reflection.

Someone rapped imperiously on her door, and her newfound boldness threatened to take a nosedive as her mind was suddenly flooded with memories of that spine-melting kiss. Her cheeks flamed, and her breath caught in anticipation.

She shook her head in disgust. She was being ridiculous again. He was just a man, for pete's sake. Hadn't she just told herself that Kit was not so very different from any other good-looking guy? So why was she acting like a starstruck teenager?

She jerked open the cottage door so abruptly that Kit's smile was quizzical when she found him standing on her doorstep, looking fit and gorgeous in a red, white and blue color-blocked T-shirt and navy shorts that showed off long, tanned legs.

"Good morning," he said in that deep, smooth voice, giving her that same rather dangerous smile that had curled her toes last night.

Just another man? Yeah, right.

Savannah made herself breathe again, hoping her voice didn't come out in an embarrassing squeak when she replied, "Good morning."

Be very careful, Savannah, said the old, familiar voice of caution, while that new, wicked little voice urged, *Go for it.*

Ignoring both of the annoying voices in her head, Savannah lifted her chin, gave Kit a bright smile and stepped through her door.

"Ready?" she asked him.

He reached out to run a fingertip down her cheek, the touch fleeting and very light, but still enough to reignite that banked flame deep inside her.

"I'm more than ready," he assured her huskily.

Oh, Savannah, her own voice whispered inside her dazed head. *You're headed for trouble.*

2

HE COULDN'T STOP staring at her.

Kit was barely conscious of the staff efficiently working the tables or the other diners around them. All he saw was Savannah, sitting across from him and eating her breakfast with a visible appreciation that made him ache to discover if all her appetites were as enthusiastic.

He wanted her. Maybe he had from the moment he'd first seen her. He couldn't remember ever wanting a woman this fast, this strongly, this powerfully after such a brief time.

He didn't even know her, he reminded himself.

And then she smiled at him over the rim of a glass of freshly squeezed orange juice and the hunger hit him again. Hard.

Whoever she was, he wanted her.

How long should he wait before he could tell her so without scaring her away?

He'd had trouble getting her to talk at first. She'd seemed to have a bit of difficulty meeting his eyes across the table, and he suspected that she was remembering that incredible kiss they'd shared before parting last night. He hadn't meant to kiss her quite so thoroughly. He'd intended only to allow himself a quick taste of her, something he'd been wanting to do for hours on the dance floor. But the kiss had flared out of control almost before he'd realized what was happening.

It had been all he could do to pull back last night. To keep himself from sweeping her into his arms and carrying her inside her cabin and straight to bed. Only the knowledge that she hadn't been ready, that it was much too soon, that he would ruin everything if he gave in to the impulse, had given him the strength to turn and walk away, before the quick flare of panic he'd seen in her eyes prompted her to cancel their plans for today.

She seemed to be relaxing a bit with him now. They'd discovered a mutual passion for old movies—particularly musicals—and that had given Savannah renewed confidence with him.

He could listen to her talk all day, he thought, finding himself gazing across the table at her again. He had no idea what he'd eaten, but he knew that Savannah liked Cary Grant better than Clark Gable, that she had wanted to grow up to be Leslie Caron, that she would happily watch any movie that starred Gene Kelly or Bing Crosby, and that she preferred old comedies and musicals to the tearjerkers typical of the Bette Davis and Joan Crawford era.

"The sillier the premise, the more I seem to like it," she confessed wryly. "I'm a movie critic's nightmare."

"Maybe," he agreed with a chuckle. "But you're a movie producer's dream. Have you checked the premises of the big blockbusters this summer? We aren't talking rocket science."

"If I wanted rocket science, I would read a science journal. I watch movies for fun and escapism, usually, though I can appreciate a truly serious film when I'm in the mood for one."

"So," he asked a bit too casually, "do you like adventure films? You know, flying bullets and two-fisted heroes?"

What Kit really wanted to know was whether Savannah was really unaware of who he was, what he did for a living. She seemed to have no idea that he was Christopher Pace, award-winning novelist and screenwriter. He'd suspected last night that she didn't have a clue about his identity, and he'd found that refreshing, especially after the hectic pace of the past couple of years. It was nice to be with someone who didn't seem to want anything from him, who seemed more interested in what he had to say than in who he knew or how much money he made.

It was nice to be with Savannah.

"I like them sometimes," she replied, bringing his attention back to their conversation. "As long as they don't get too blatantly gory. And especially if the two-fisted hero falls for an equally dashing heroine during the escapade. But I tend to watch more of the old movies on TV than the newer releases. I always seem to be too busy to get to a theater, but I often have the television set on while I do other things in the evenings."

"What do you do?" he asked, wondering why she stayed so busy. He'd already pegged her as a successful, professional woman. He assumed she was taking a solitary vacation for the same reason he was—because she'd needed a quiet break to ward off total exhaustion.

"I make a living," she answered with a shrug. "But I don't want to think about work right now."

"Neither do I," he seconded immediately, a little relieved.

There was plenty of time to talk about real life, he

thought in satisfaction. For now, he was simply enjoying being with her.

SAVANNAH FOUND Kit's total attention to her both flattering and unnerving. Every time she glanced up from her meal, she found him looking at her. He listened closely to every word she said, making her feel that her words were interesting, important.

A striking redhead in a microscopic bikini passed by just on the other side of the glass wall, and Kit didn't even seem to notice, though every other male head in the vicinity swiveled to follow her. Savannah couldn't help remembering the way Vince had always watched every other girl around, making her feel slighted, unimportant. Other men she'd dated had behaved the same way. But not Kit.

No man had ever made Savannah feel so special. She found herself falling a little harder for him each moment they were together, but her reckless side insisted it was okay. Last night, after Kit had gone, she'd decided she *could* handle this...as long as she kept reminding herself that it wouldn't last. She could enjoy being with Kit, even fall a little in love with him—as long as she didn't let herself start to believe in the fantasy.

This vacation would be a memory she could treasure, that she could pull out and savor when she found herself alone and lonely, nights in the future, she promised herself. She wouldn't lament the inevitable ending, but would rejoice, instead, that she'd had this experience just once before she settled comfortably into her thirties, directing all her energy into the hair-raising task of raising two active teenagers.

I deserve this, she thought with just a touch of the old

defiance. After thirteen years of being cautious and dependable and utterly predictable, she deserved this time just for herself. A chance to feel young again, and pretty, and desirable, and daring.

All the things she felt when Kit smiled at her.

AFTER BREAKFAST, as they stepped outside the restaurant, Savannah turned her face upward and closed her eyes for a moment, soaking in the sun and fresh air like a tropical plant that had been confined indoors all winter.

She opened her eyes to find Kit standing close, looking at her again. She smiled.

"It's so beautiful here."

He cleared his throat. "Yes," he agreed without taking his gaze from her face.

She felt a blush stain her cheeks.

Kit reached out to take her hand. "Walk with me."

Even as Savannah wound her fingers with his and fell into step beside him, she wondered if anyone ever turned this man down. He had a way of making requests that didn't leave a lot of room for discussion.

Savannah had been very careful to avoid arrogant and overbearing men since Vince Hankins. She wondered if those tendencies didn't lurk behind Kit's charming, attractive exterior. It occurred to her that even in fiction, gentlemen pirates could be ruthless when crossed, relentless when in pursuit of something they wanted.

But then she shook those nervous, fanciful thoughts away, telling herself she was being ridiculous.

"Where are we going?" she asked, as Kit led her around the main compound and along a flower-lined path that led upward toward the high center of the island.

He smiled down at her. "Does it matter?"

When he looked at her like that, she would willingly follow him anywhere, she realized dazedly. "No. It doesn't matter."

His smile deepened. He tucked her hand into the crook of his elbow, and matched his steps to hers on the well-worn path. She couldn't resist spreading her fingers over his bare arm, testing the muscles beneath his skin, feeling the brush of hair against her palm. She couldn't help imagining what it would be like to run her hand over all his skin, or wondering if his chest was sleek or hairy.

How could she care where he led her as long as they were walking this closely together? She lifted her eyes to his face, and found he was watching her again. She could almost imagine that he was reading her thoughts.

He seemed to know where he was going, so she paid little attention to the twists and turns the path took. She did notice, however, when they reached a low chain across the path, and a sign that clearly said Do Not Enter—in several languages.

Kit stepped over the chain and held his hand out to Savannah, silently inviting her to follow him.

She lifted an eyebrow. "You don't read English? Or French, or Spanish, or—"

"I know what the sign says," he assured her. "In all the languages. Come on. I want to show you something."

"But—"

"Don't worry about it. The owner is a friend of mine. I've been up here before."

He laughed softly at her skeptical expression. "You don't believe me?" At her sheepish shrug, he added, "Tell you what. If we get into trouble, I'll nobly take the blame. I'll claim that I kidnapped you and forced you up this path under threat of dire consequences."

She couldn't help smiling. "What dire consequences?"

"A fate worse than death," he assured her. "You can tell them I threatened to ravish you."

Savannah's cheeks burned. Being ravished by Kit didn't seem like such a terrible fate, at all.

She cleared her throat. "You're sure this is okay with the owner?"

He nodded, his hand still extended to her. "Trust me."

She seemed to have no choice. She placed her hand in his in a gesture that was becoming intriguingly familiar.

This path, though clearly marked, was obviously not as well-traveled as the public walkways. Flowers and vines crowded the edges, and more than once Kit had to move a heavy palm frond out of the way so that Savannah could slip beneath it. The ground climbed rather sharply under their feet, and she was grateful for Kit's steadying hand.

Just where *was* he taking her?

At last they slipped through another curtain of greenery and Savannah's breath caught sharply in her throat.

"Kit! This is spectacular."

He smiled smugly and stood to one side so that she could take full advantage of the breathtaking view from the edge of the bluff at which the private path ended.

This was probably the highest point on the island, Savannah realized in wonder, gazing at the exquisite scenery spread out below them. They could almost see the entire resort from here—the neat little cottages, the two waterfall-accented swimming pools, the tennis courts and stables, the beach with its colorful splattering of umbrellas and convenient drink stands.

Tiny white Jeeps that looked like toys from where they stood darted around the resort, carrying guests to the shuttle launches to the larger shopping-and-casino islands nearby, transporting employees from the main resort to the separate staff village that Savannah knew lay at the far end of the island. And at the horizon, endless blue water melded into endless blue sky, effectively creating the illusion that no world existed beyond this one.

"No wonder the owner wants to keep this spot for himself," she murmured. "I've never seen anything more beautiful in my life."

"Neither have I."

Kit's voice was gruff. Deep. And very, very close.

She turned to find him standing only inches away from her, his gaze devouring her face.

She shivered and twisted her fingers in front of her. She tried to smile. "You're always staring at me," she accused, trying to make light of it.

He didn't return the smile. Instead, he answered her with her own words. "I've never seen anything more beautiful in my life."

She almost moaned. How could she possibly be sensible when he said things like that?

She couldn't.

She didn't try to resist when he reached for her. He moved slowly, as though making an effort not to startle her, but she could have assured him there was no need.

She wasn't afraid of him. Maybe she should have been afraid—or at least wary of the feelings he aroused in her—but she wasn't.

Looking up into his dark eyes, she saw herself reflected there, saw the wonder and curiosity on her own face. She lifted a hand to his smooth-shaven cheek, thinking again that he was the most gorgeous man she'd ever seen. He had the dark, polished, cleanly chiseled look that heroes had in the old movies, the kind of face the cameras loved, and yet he seemed so real, so touchable.

Kit stood very still, letting her study him, explore his face with the tips of her fingers. He seemed to be holding his breath, as if his patience and restraint were hard-won. She felt the faintest quiver go through him when she trailed her hand down his throat and across his broad chest. That involuntary reaction on his part gave her the courage to move closer and lift her mouth invitingly toward his.

Kit didn't waste any time taking her up on her silent offer. His mouth came down on hers with a force that rocked her back on her heels. Savannah locked her arms around his neck for support, bringing her into full contact with his long, hard body, her breasts flattened against his chest, her bare legs tangled with his. His hands slid down her back, pressing, shaping, holding her close.

He wanted her.

The evidence was unmistakable. The sensation unbelievable. Heady. Electrifying. More intoxicating than the fine champagne they'd shared the night before.

He wanted her with a grown man's passion, with an

honesty and an intensity that she found almost irresistible. He was doing wonders for her feminine ego, which had taken so many hits during the past years, and she was immeasurably grateful to him for giving her back something she'd thought irrevocably lost. A sense of her own desirability and her own worth, apart from her family and her commitments.

He was giving her back herself. And even if she didn't really know him, she couldn't helping loving him for it. *At least a little,* she thought, tilting her head to allow him to deepen the kiss.

His tongue thrust eagerly between her lips and swept the inside of her mouth with a thoroughness that thrilled her. Tentatively, and then more confidently, she responded in kind.

Oh, he tasted good. Warm. Spicy. Male.

He moved slightly against her, fanning the fire inside her. A heavy ache throbbed between her thighs, and she pressed closer to the answering hardness between his.

Kit groaned and cupped her hips to hold her more firmly against him.

"Savannah," he gasped, tearing his mouth from hers to allow them oxygen. "Do you have any idea what you're doing to me?"

Oh, yes, she knew exactly what she was doing. Even if she hadn't felt his arousal against her abdomen, she could see it in the hot flush on his cheeks, hear it in the ragged edge to his breathing, feel it in the tremors that ran through him.

And she laughed in sheer exhilaration, feeling freer and more alive than she'd felt in years.

In response to Savannah's laughter, the corners of Kit's mouth kicked up into his wicked, pirate's grin. He lifted her off the ground and spun her until she was clinging to him helplessly, laughing and begging him to stop.

"That'll teach you to laugh at me," he said with exaggerated fierceness as he set her back on her feet.

She had to cling to him for support until the scenery stopped whirling around her.

"You," she said breathlessly, "are dangerous."

His expression turned abruptly tender. He cupped her face between his hands. "Not to you, sweetheart," he assured her gruffly.

And he kissed her again, this time so sweetly that it brought a hard lump to her throat.

She fell just a little more deeply.

"Hey, can't you read, buddy? This place is off-limits to the guests."

The unexpected voice was a low, menacing growl, making Savannah gulp and draw quickly back from Kit.

The intruder looked as dangerous as his voice. His hair was midnight-black, his narrowed eyes obsidian, his features dark and formidable. Well over six feet of solid muscle had been packed into a thin white shirt and loose white slacks.

Kit tilted his head arrogantly and met the other man's challenging gaze. "What are you going to do? Throw me off the bluff?"

"I just might," the man in white drawled, sounding entirely serious.

Savannah thought maybe it was time for her to intercede before the testosterone levels built to an explosive level.

"It's okay," she assured the newcomer, speaking

with a breezy confidence she had to fake. "Kit's a friend of the resort owner."

The man raked his dark eyes slowly across Kit's face. "Is that right?"

Kit glanced down at Savannah. "Er—did I say I was a *friend* of the owner?"

Oh, great. He'd lied to her, and now they were both in trouble. She glared at him. "Yes. That's what you said."

The other man heaved a heavy sigh and shook his head. "Trying to impress a pretty woman by claiming friendship with me again, Kit? How many times do I have to tell you not to do that?"

Savannah had just figured out that she'd been snowed when both men broke into dopey grins.

"Savannah," Kit said. "This is Rafe. He likes to pretend he's the supreme ruler of this little island of his. A Napoleon complex, you understand."

Rafe's reply was low-voiced and mildly obscene, from what Savannah could hear of it.

Leaving Kit chuckling, Rafe Dancer turned courteously to Savannah. "I can have security here in moments if this man is bothering you, ma'am," he assured her.

A reluctant smile tugged at Savannah's mouth. "No, I think I can handle him," she lied. "But thank you for the offer."

"It's my job to make sure my guests are comfortable," he replied smoothly.

"We'll be sure and let you know if we need anything," Kit said, his tone rather arrogantly dismissive.

Rafe only lifted an eyebrow. "I meant my *valued* guests, of course," he remarked, making it clear that Kit did not fit into that category.

Kit only laughed and shook his head. "I never could get the last word with this guy," he said to Savannah.

"I hope you're enjoying your stay at the resort, Ms.—er—"

"Savannah," she corrected him with a smile. "And, yes, thank you, I'm having a wonderful time."

He inclined his head, apparently satisfied with her reply. "Then I'll let you get back to it. Don't hesitate to let me or one of my staff know if there's anything you need. Kit, I'll be seeing you later."

The words seemed to hold as much warning as promise. And then Rafe Dancer slipped away into the greenery, as swiftly and silently as he'd approached.

Blinking, Savannah turned back to Kit.

"Forgive me, but your friend is a bit scary," she said frankly.

He laughed. "If you think *he's* scary, you should meet his wife. And their two-year-old terror of a son."

Savannah was rather surprised to think of the man she'd just met as the father of a toddler. And then she remembered the warmth of his flashing smile and decided that maybe she could imagine it, after all.

"Okay, what are we going to do now? Shall we make passionate love in the bushes or go for a swim?"

Savannah whipped her head up and stared at Kit, not at all certain she'd heard him correctly.

His devilish expression confirmed that he'd said exactly what she'd thought he'd said.

She gave him a quelling frown, though she had to fight an answering smile. "Let's go for a swim."

He sighed deeply. "If you insist."

He would never know how tempted she'd been to pull him into the bushes and take him up on his other suggestion, Savannah decided, resisting an urge to fan her overheated face with her hand.

3

IT WAS EARLY EVENING by the time Kit left Savannah at her door to shower and change for dinner. She entered the cottage with a smile that felt permanently etched on her face.

She'd had a wonderful afternoon with Kit. A picnic on the beach, followed by an afternoon of playful flirtation in the delightfully cool ocean waves. And when he had taken her into his arms and kissed her, with salt water clinging to their lips and dripping down their faces, she'd forgotten about anyone who might be watching as she wrapped her arms around his neck and pressed her wet body close to his to kiss him back.

She moved slowly toward the shower, replaying every moment of the afternoon in her mind, carefully storing the memories. She never wanted to forget the way Kit had looked, stretched out on a beach blanket, the tropical sun washing over his delectable bare chest, glittering in his coffee-colored hair, gleaming in his wicked dark eyes. She'd nearly swallowed her tongue every time she'd looked at him.

He was the most beautiful man she'd ever seen. But it wasn't only his appearance that drew her to him, she realized. She enjoyed being with him. She liked him, very much.

Maybe she even more than liked him.

But she refused to allow herself to indulge in *if only*...

She turned on the shower, then reached behind her ear to remove the splashy red flower Kit had impulsively tucked there while walking her back from the beach. He'd assured her gravely that Rafe wouldn't mind that he'd picked just one of the many brilliant blooms on the island.

"Especially," he'd added, "if he could see how pretty it looks on you."

And then he had kissed her again.

Swallowing hard, Savannah set the flower on the sink and stepped into the shower. The cool water did very little to reduce the heat that last kiss had left smoldering in her.

KIT FELT GREAT as he sauntered across the resort compound toward his cottage, where he intended to take a shower and then make a few calls that he'd been putting off for the past couple of days. He would only be killing time until he could be with Savannah again, he thought with a surge of eagerness that he found both wryly amusing and a bit unnerving.

What, exactly, was going on between the two of them? What was it she made him feel? Whatever it was, it was powerful. Incredible. Like nothing he'd ever felt before.

Something in her eyes got to him in a way that no one ever had before. There was a sweetness...almost an innocence...in their brilliant blue depths that contrasted intriguingly with the air of maturity and hard-earned experience that she projected at times. He was fascinated by the way she changed so mercurially from cautious to reckless, from a bit shy to delightfully bold, from guarded to stunningly passionate.

Everything about her fascinated him. And he couldn't wait to learn even more.

He let himself into his cottage and pulled his slightly sticky T-shirt over his head, tossing it over a wicker chair. The cottage was clean, welcoming, and impeccably furnished. Only the best would do for Rafe Dancer's guests, Kit thought with a smile.

Rafe certainly had it made these days. A home in paradise, a staff of loyal employees who waited on him hand and foot, a beautiful, intelligent wife, and a cute, healthy kid. A big change from when Kit had first met him eight years ago, while doing research for his first novel.

Rafe had been with the Drug Enforcement Agency then. Kit had found Rafe to be a hard, stern, dangerous man who rarely smiled. A loner. And yet, Kit had liked him. They'd become casual friends during the weeks they'd worked together, and had kept in touch sporadically since. When Rafe had left the DEA to open this resort, Kit had been given a standing invitation to visit. This was the second time he'd taken Rafe up on the offer.

He hadn't enjoyed himself nearly this much the last time. Savannah hadn't been here then.

Kit thought of the quizzical look in Rafe's eyes when he'd found Kit kissing Savannah. He was tempted to go look up his friend and ask him if this was the way Rafe had felt when he'd first met T.J. Harris, the hot-tempered, smart-mouthed reporter Rafe had rescued and then married.

But something stopped him. Kit wasn't quite ready to talk about Savannah yet, not even to Rafe. After all, what could he say? That he'd spotted the woman sitting on a beach, and hadn't been able to look away from her since? That he had danced with her and felt as if he'd finally found the partner he'd been searching for all his life? That he'd fallen damned hard for her, even before learning her last name?

No. He couldn't say any of that now. He wanted to wait, spend more time with her, find out if these feelings were really as special as they seemed.

And yet he couldn't help thinking that Rafe would understand. After more than three years, Rafe was still visibly in love with his wife, and proudly devoted to their young son. He was content in a way that he had not been when Kit first met him.

And if that could happen for Rafe Dancer, it could happen for anyone. Even him.

SAVANNAH HUNG UP the telephone harder than she'd intended, making it jingle in objection. She could still hear the echoes of her mother's cool voice. Although everything at home was fine, Savannah's mother still disapproved of Savannah's decision to take this vacation. Words like "irresponsible" and "selfish" had marked her conversation, along with questions like, "What if something goes wrong here while you're off lying in the sun and pampering yourself? How can you enjoy yourself when you're so far from your family?"

Seething with resentment at the unfairness of her mother's accusations, Savannah brushed her hair with rapid, choppy strokes.

"Selfish," she muttered. "Irresponsible. I can't believe she would talk to me that way."

Savannah had become a pattern card of responsibility. For the past thirteen years she had worked and struggled and taken care of everyone but herself. While she didn't begrudge the things she'd done for her family, and would never regret having her children, she couldn't help missing the carefree, youthful years she'd lost. She refused to feel guilty for taking a few days to relax and have fun, especially since she hadn't been needed at home this week, despite her mother's innuendos to the contrary.

She didn't even want to think about what her mother would have said if she'd seen Savannah plastered intimately all over a man who was still a virtual stranger to her.

She looked into the mirror as she applied her lipstick, involuntarily taking note of the fine lines just developing at the corners of her eyes. She thought of her approaching thirtieth birthday. Though objectively she knew she was still young, thirty suddenly seemed old. Maybe because she'd had to give up her childhood so abruptly, had been forced into the responsibilities of adulthood before she'd been quite ready to take them on.

She wasn't unhappy in her life—far from it, she assured herself as she glanced at the silver-framed photograph of the twins on her nightstand. It was only this approaching birthday that had her down, she decided. From what she'd heard, most women found their thirtieth birthday unsettling.

All she was asking was one last carefree night before she returned to the stressful, but usually rewarding, routines of her life back home. A lighthearted, private farewell to her twenties. And what could be better than to share it with a charming, utterly gorgeous man who made her feel young, beautiful...and desirable.

A couple of taps on her door made her look quickly into the mirror for one last check of her appearance. She'd left her hair down, soft and loose around her shoulders, which were bare beneath the narrow straps of her cream-colored dress. The rather low-cut garment fit smoothly across her full bust, skimmed her waist and hips, then flared into a flirty, floating hem just above her knees.

One more night, she promised the two smiling faces in the nightstand photograph. *That's all I'm asking.*

And then she hurried across the room and opened the door. Her breath caught in her throat when she saw that Kit had chosen to wear exquisitely tailored pale gray slacks and a loose-fitting ice-blue shirt that draped softly over his well-proportioned shoulders and chest. He looked almost too good to be real.

"I've brought you something," he murmured, holding out his hand.

A bit warily, she took the little resort gift-shop box and lifted the lid. And then she smiled.

The box held a small gold pin shaped like one of the tropical flowers she'd so admired on the island. The petals had been lacquered a brilliant crimson, the leaves a rich green. It looked so real that Savannah could almost smell the flower's scent.

"This is lovely, Kit," she said, wondering if she should accept this gift from a man who was still technically a stranger to her.

"It made me think of you," he replied, looking pleased with her expression. "I wanted you to have it as a souvenir."

A souvenir. Something to remember him by—as if she could ever forget this man.

Impulsively, Savannah tightened her fingers around the box and made her decision. "Thank you."

"You're welcome. Let's go dance, shall we?"

Without further hesitation, she allowed herself to slide back into the fantasy.

KIT COULDN'T KEEP his eyes off Savannah again that evening. She looked so beautiful. Her dark blond hair gleamed in the candlelight that was reflected in her vivid blue eyes. Her flirty dress bared her smooth throat and shoulders, showing just a hint of soft cleavage. Her legs were long and slim, and she moved gracefully on her high-heeled sandals.

Beauty. Intelligence. Maturity. Wit. An appreciation for classic tunes and films. Kit was beginning to wonder if she could possibly be real.

She hadn't exactly been forthcoming about herself. There was so much he wanted to know about her. So many questions he wanted to ask. Her last name, for example. Her hometown. Her career. Her background. Whether he was going to have to fight another man to win her.

Wryly amused at his raging curiosity, Kit forced himself to be patient. There would be plenty of time for questions, he promised himself. But tonight there was music to dance to, champagne to savor, a tropical moon to smile over them. The night was pure magic, and he didn't want to waste a moment of it. He, more than anyone, knew how rapidly illusion faded into reality.

The orchestra played a sultry version of "Moonlight in Vermont," utilizing the talents of its brilliant pianist. Kit swayed slowly with Savannah in his arms, their gazes locked, their smiles intimate. He made a few tight turns and she matched his steps precisely, as if they'd danced together for years. Gently, he swung her away from him, twirled her beneath his upraised arm, then pulled her back against his chest.

She laughed softly and rested her cheek against his shoulder. "I didn't know I could dance like this until I danced with you," she confessed.

He liked the sound of that—as though no one else had ever really danced with her before him. He almost winced at how possessive he felt at the thought. He certainly had no right to be possessive about this woman he hardly knew. But he wasn't at all sure he could help it. At least not tonight.

He forced himself to answer lightly. "I guess all those dancing lessons my mom forced me to take paid off."

"Obviously a very wise woman."

"She's amazing. I was very lucky to have been raised by her."

"It's nice that you and your mother are so close."

Kit thought there was a touch of wistfulness in Savannah's words. Was she not close to her own mother? Or had her mother, perhaps, passed away?

He wished he knew her well enough to ask without seeming to pry.

Instead he said only, "My mom would like you."

He felt Savannah stiffen almost imperceptibly. She didn't respond.

An older couple, in their late sixties perhaps, danced closer and smiled at Kit and Savannah. "We were just saying how nice it is to see a young couple who enjoy the old songs," the woman said. "And who know how to dance to them."

Kit smiled at the woman in return. "How could we not enjoy this?" he asked as the orchestra played "What'll I Do?"

"Lot of young people your age are out contorting themselves to all that new garbage," the older man drawled in disapproval. "Hasn't been any real music written since 1954."

"Now, Gus, that's not quite true. Elvis didn't even get started until 1956," he wife reminded him as they danced further away from Kit and Savannah.

"Well, yeah," her husband admitted. "I wasn't countin' Elvis, of course."

Kit grinned down at Savannah when the other couple was out of earshot, and noticed that she was struggling not to laugh. "Did that accent sound a bit familiar?" he asked.

"I'd say they were from Mississippi," she replied with exaggerated haughtiness. "*I'm* from Georgia."

He was delighted to have learned something new about her, even in such a roundabout way. "I should have noticed the difference immediately."

"Of course. There's no similarity whatsoever." She gave the latter two words at least a half dozen extra syllables, making him grin.

Damn, but he was glad he'd come to Serendipity.

HAND IN HAND, Savannah and Kit walked along the deserted beach in the moonlight, their shoes dangling from their free hands. Savannah couldn't help thinking that it was like a scene from a romantic movie. A fragrant tropical breeze, surf lapping at her bare toes, a gorgeous man at her side.

What a lovely memory this would make when she returned to reality, she thought with a bittersweet pang.

Kit smiled down at her. "It's getting late."

"Yes."

"I don't want the night to end," he confessed.

She sighed lightly. "Neither do I."

But of course it would end. Fantasies couldn't last forever.

"Maybe tomorrow we can go sightseeing or something," he suggested.

Tomorrow she would be gone. This was her last night on the island, and she would be on a launch that departed in the morning before most of the guests were even awake. She started to tell Kit so, but something made her fall silent. It had been such a perfect evening, after such a perfect day. She didn't want it to end with awkward goodbyes.

Instead, all she said was, "Perhaps."

Kit seemed satisfied with her answer. He began to hum as they strolled along the damp sand.

"'Star Dust'," she murmured with a smile.

He grinned, then impulsively turned and took her into his arms, startling her into dropping her shoes. His fell beside them. Still humming, he guided her into an impromptu dance. Savannah laughed and cooperated.

This had to be the most romantic man she'd ever met.

He probably treated many women this way, a practical little voice in her mind warned. Took them on picnics, gave them flowers, danced with them in the moonlight. Heck, he might even do it for a living.

She didn't care. Tonight, she didn't want to know.

She didn't even consider protesting when he drew her into his arms for a long, deep kiss that was as perfect as the rest of the evening had been.

The laughter died inside her. Desire took its place.

Every time Kit kissed her, her reactions to him were stronger. The more time she spent with him, the harder she fell for him, and it seemed only natural to want to pursue that overwhelming attraction to its inevitable outcome.

Deep inside, she was aware of a sense of amazement that she was standing here kissing him this way, right out in the open where anyone could see them.

No one here knew her. No one cared what she did. Nothing she did could possibly come back to haunt her.

The realization was liberating.

She wrapped her arms around Kit's neck and kissed him exactly the way she'd been wanting to kiss him from the first time he'd taken her in his arms on the dance floor. With absolutely nothing held back.

A groan rumbled deep in Kit's chest, vibrating against Savannah's breasts.

Kit cupped her face in his hands, and scattered kisses across her face. Her cheeks. Her nose. Her chin.

"Let's go back," he murmured, his voice rough.

She knew where he meant. Back to the compound. Back to the cottages—hers or his. They had been leading up to this all day.

I want him, she thought, drawing back to look up at his moonlight-silvered face, his dark, intense eyes. She'd never wanted another man this way. For all she knew, she might never feel like this again. Tonight could be her last chance to know true passion.

He held out his hand. She noted that it wasn't quite steady, and it touched her that he didn't seem to be taking this any more casually than she was. She wanted to believe that this connection between them was as wondrous, as unique, as completely unexpected for Kit as it was for her.

She hadn't come to Serendipity Island to fall in love.

But she had, at least a little. Would it really be so wrong for her to give herself this one night with this incredible man?

No one would ever have to know. It would be her own private birthday present to herself. An adventure to savor, a memory to treasure, an experience never to be repeated.

She slipped her hand into his.

Savannah sighed as she and Kit walked slowly toward the guest cottages, using the full moon and discreetly placed security lights to guide their way. It was well after midnight, but she wasn't tired. Far from it, in fact. She felt wide awake.

All her senses seemed heightened. The night looked more beautiful than any she could remember. The air smelled sweeter. The breeze felt incredibly sensual against her face. Kit's hand was warm and strong around hers.

"Magic," she murmured.

"What was that?"

She smiled up at him. "Magic," she repeated. "This night seems too perfect to be real."

He lifted her hand to his lips. "I was just thinking much the same about you. Almost too perfect to be real."

Savannah shook her head, disturbed by his words. "I'm far from perfect."

"You couldn't convince me of that."

She glanced away from him. "That's because you don't really know me."

"I'm hoping to remedy that soon."

She knew this was the time to tell him that she would be leaving early the next morning. That there would be no chance for them to know each other better.

She suspected that Kit would be very surprised to discover that the real Savannah McBride was very different from the woman she'd allowed herself to be on the island. She doubted very much that he would continue to be interested in a woman with as many commitments and responsibilities as she had. Other men had been intrigued at first by her appearance, but they hadn't been interested in the baggage she would bring with her into a relationship.

She'd been right, she decided again. It would be best if she kept quiet about her departure plans.

Kit paused outside his own cottage. "I have champagne inside," he said invitingly. "Will you have one last drink with me this evening?"

One last drink with him. Period. There would be no others. Savannah's chest tightened with what might have been grief, but she forced it down, reminding herself that she intended to have no regrets. "Yes, I'd like that," she said.

Kit unlocked his door.

Savannah swallowed hard before she stepped through it.

Kit's living area looked much like her own, Savannah noted, wiping her suddenly damp palms surreptitiously on her skirt. He'd left the overhead light off in favor of the soft illumination from a lamp beside the sofa. The dim light cast deep shadows in the corners, making the room appear smaller and more intimate.

The shirt Kit had worn earlier lay over the back of a chair. She pictured him peeling it over his head and tossing it there, and the image made her mouth go dry.

"Did you say you have champagne?" she asked, her voice sounding a bit odd in her ears.

Kit smiled and nodded. "Have a seat," he said, motioning toward the deep-cushioned sofa. "I'll get it."

The small wet bar was tucked discreetly into one corner of the room. He stopped on his way to turn on the stereo unit. When Nat King Cole began to croon "Unforgettable," Savannah realized Kit had already loaded the CD changer with old standards.

But she didn't need a song to remind her that she would never forget this night.

Or Kit.

He filled two champagne glasses, then carried them back to where she sat on the sofa—perched as far to one side as she could possibly fit.

Ignoring the other end of the sofa, he sat close to her, draping his right arm behind her and holding his glass in his left hand. He held his glass out toward her.

"To magic," he murmured.

She touched her glass to his, making an effort to hold it steady. And then she lifted it rather desperately to her lips.

Kit watched her, taking a more sedate sip of his own wine. "Trying to find courage in that glass, Savannah?"

She cleared her throat and avoided his eyes. "I was thirsty."

He took her glass out of her hands and set it on the table beside his, giving her little chance to resist. And then he placed a hand on her cheek and turned her face toward his, so that she had no choice but to look at him.

"Are you afraid of me?"

His question was blunt, yet it held an undertone of tenderness.

She twisted her fingers in her lap. "Of course not."

She wasn't afraid of Kit, she assured herself. She was

afraid of herself, perhaps, and the way she reacted to him. Afraid of the feelings he aroused in her. Afraid that he would haunt her for the rest of her life. But she wasn't afraid of him...at least, not very much.

He stroked the side of his finger down her cheek. His skin felt so warm against hers. She wondered if hers felt icy to him.

"You are so beautiful," he murmured.

She wasn't quite comfortable with his compliment. Being pretty had been her biggest asset in high school. It was because she'd been pretty that the boys had wanted to be with her. Her face and figure had been what had attracted Vince to her; he'd liked the way she looked hanging on his arm.

It annoyed her that she thought of Vince now. This was her fantasy, she reminded herself as Kit lowered his mouth slowly toward hers. Her private, secret celebration of everything she'd put behind her, of all she'd become.

She'd chosen to be here. And she would be an idiot not to make the most of it, she told herself as she allowed her hands to slide up Kit's chest and around his shoulders.

The CD player was set on random play. An instrumental version of "Isn't It Romantic?" swelled through the room.

Against her lips, Kit murmured, "Don't be afraid, Savannah. Can't you feel how very right this is?"

Nothing had ever felt more right to her.

Kit made love to her mouth while his hand slid down her bare arm and then moved to her thigh. She felt his warmth through the filmy fabric of her dress, and an answering heat pooled inside her.

He shifted his weight so that he was leaning over

her. Murmuring endearments, he buried his face in her throat, nibbling at the skin there until she arched beneath him, her entire body tingling. His legs tangled with hers, the crisp fabric of his slacks deliciously rough against her bare skin. Her full skirt foamed around them. Kit's fingers slipped beneath the hem, sliding up her thigh toward her hip.

Savannah shifted involuntarily closer to him, longing for him to touch her more intimately. Aching to feel his hands on her, his skin pressed to hers. Without stopping to think about her actions, she fumbled with the buttons of his shirt.

She had to bite back a moan when she was finally able to spread her hands across his bare chest. She felt his muscles contracting sharply beneath her fingertips. Felt the hardness pressing greedily against her thigh.

She wanted him inside her, so closely entwined with her that she wouldn't know where she stopped and he began. She wanted to feel sensations she'd never felt before, wanted to know the kind of passion she'd only fantasized about until now.

Kit could give her those things. She couldn't have created a more perfect fantasy lover had she tried.

Beneath her skirt, his fingers slid across her stomach, and brushed across the part of her that throbbed with need.

She gasped.

He nuzzled against the low neckline of her dress, pushing the fabric out of the way to bare the top of her breast. His mouth was avid, his breath warm on her chilled flesh. He slid the tip of his tongue along the lace edge of her scanty bra, just missing her distended nipple.

She shuddered helplessly.

"Savannah." Kit's voice was hardly recognizable. He drew back to gaze down at her, and his face was flushed, his eyes glittering with an almost feral intensity. His chest heaved with his ragged breathing, and she knew his need matched her own.

The air around them seemed to crackle and sizzle with the heat they'd generated. This had been building between them from the time their eyes had met. Savannah wasn't certain she could control it now, even if she tried.

"I want you," he said, and there was a man's raw, possessive hunger in his words.

Panic shot through her, and she froze beneath him. Suddenly this moment seemed too strong, too real.

What was she doing?

4

KIT'S EYES narrowed, as they swiftly searched her face. He groaned.

"Don't do this," he grated, half command, half plea. "Not now."

He crushed her mouth beneath his again, lifting her into him. She felt the power in his arms, the sheer strength of him. And now she shivered in desire as well as fear.

"Don't be afraid of me," he whispered, feathering kisses across her temple. "I would never hurt you, Savannah."

She looked up at him, and she realized with staggering abruptness what a fool she'd been.

Kit wasn't a fantasy. He was a man. A strong, virile, healthy male whose borderline-arrogant self-assurance had already made her think of him as a pirate on more than one occasion.

Pirates, she reminded herself, didn't like to be refused when there was something they wanted. It wasn't the first time the thought had crossed her mind.

Why hadn't she paid more attention to her own mental warnings?

She'd tried to convince herself she was in love with him. Tried to rationalize her behavior with romantic fantasies. Now she couldn't be sure whether what she had felt was love or mere lust. And that uncertainty was an all-too-painful reminder of her past.

"Kit, I—I don't think I can do this," she said, forcing her voice through the knot of mingled remorse and anxiety in her throat.

"Sure you can," he replied bracingly, burying his fingers in her tumbled hair. "There's nothing stopping us."

He suddenly stiffened, and looked down at her with a frown. "You aren't—tell me you aren't married."

"I'm not married," she complied. "I never have been. But—"

He let out a deep breath of relief.

"Oh, man. That shook me for a minute," he admitted. And then he slanted his pirate's smile at her again and started to gather her close. "So there's absolutely no reason we can't—"

"*I* can't," she repeated, using her hands on his forearms to hold herself away from him.

She hoped he wouldn't insist that she explain her sudden change of mind. She didn't think she could, even to herself. She only knew that everything had suddenly become too real to her. Too serious.

She saw the instinctive refusal in his expression, the temptation to sweep past her objections and continue where they'd left off. She couldn't help remembering Vince, thinking back to the bruises he'd given her when she'd annoyed him.

She reminded herself that she wasn't that inexperienced, insecure girl now. She would never be treated that way again.

She held Kit's gaze levelly with her own.

He studied her expression closely, and seemed to see something there that made up his mind.

He sighed and closed his eyes. She sensed the battle going on inside him. She knew that it had been hard won when the tension left his arms and he nodded and drew away.

"I'll walk you to your cottage."

She swallowed, only then admitting to herself how uncertain she'd really been about Kit's reaction to her last-minute rejection. She couldn't blame him, of course, for being annoyed with her. After all, she'd been all over him all day, she thought with a twinge of guilt.

"Kit, I—"

He spoke quickly, overriding her halting attempt at an apology. "Let's, er, not discuss it any more right now, okay?" he asked, standing to button his shirt. His movements were a bit stiff, as if he was experiencing physical discomfort.

Savannah supposed that he was, at that.

Her own body thrumming in irritable frustration, she stood and straightened her clothes. One of her shoes had fallen off; she groped for it awkwardly.

The romantic music continued to play from the other side of the room. Savannah winced when she recognized the tune. "People Will Say We're in Love."

She turned away from Kit to slip into her shoe, hiding her reaction to the number.

This wasn't at all the way she'd hoped to end her last evening with Kit, she thought regretfully. It had been such a perfect day, such a beautifully romantic evening. She'd wanted him to remember her with pleasure, not with disappointment.

THEY WALKED BACK to her cottage in silence. Savannah was peripherally aware of the beauty of their surroundings—the full moon, the starry sky, the fragrant, night-blooming flowers—but she was even more aware of Kit, walking close beside her and yet seeming very far away.

He turned to her at her door. "Are you all right?"

She moistened her lips. "Yes. I'm fine, thank you."

She didn't ask how he was. She suspected that he was still suffering from acute frustration.

She almost started to apologize again. And then she reminded herself that she had nothing to apologize for, really. She had had every right to call a halt when she'd become uncomfortable with going further.

Her caution came from experience. She'd made enough mistakes in her past. She hadn't wanted to make another one tonight.

Besides, she thought, it really was best to end the interlude between them now. No explanations. No regrets. Nothing but very sweet, very romantic memories.

It was all she dared ask of this man who was so very different from all the other men she'd known.

Kit waited until she'd unlocked her door, then touched her shoulder.

"I'll see you tomorrow," he said gently, perhaps letting her know that he wouldn't hold her rejection against her.

Savannah only smiled rather sadly in return, ignoring the nagging little voice inside her that urged her to tell him the truth about her departure plans. There was no reason to, she assured herself. Once he learned that she was gone, he would forget all about her soon enough. They didn't even know each other, really.

It wasn't as if there'd ever been any chance of anything permanent developing between them.

Given the choice, Kit would probably be no more enthusiastic about exchanging awkward goodbyes than she was, Savannah told herself.

She reached up impulsively and kissed his cheek. "Thank you for making this such a special vacation for me."

He reached for her. "Savannah—"

She took one last look at him, then turned quickly away to open her door. "Good night, Kit."

He caught her when she would have slipped inside, drew her toward him and pressed his mouth firmly, forcefully against hers for one long, thorough kiss. There was a glint of satisfaction in his eyes when he finally drew back, leaving her trembling and aching for more.

"Good night, Savannah," he said gruffly. "Dream of me."

Maybe he'd considered it an appropriately romantic line with which to conclude the evening, she thought as she closed herself into her silent cottage. But somehow his words felt more like a prediction—or a curse.

She suspected she would dream of him for years to come.

Knowing that it would be a while before she would be able to sleep—if at all—she went into the bedroom and pulled her suitcase out of the closet. She might as well pack now to save time the next morning. She would be on the first launch off the island, just after dawn.

And there would be no regrets, she assured herself. No one had been hurt. No promises broken. No dreams shattered. She'd spent a few hours with a wonderful man and, though she'd come dangerously close, she hadn't done anything foolish.

The mistakes of her past had taught her well.

AFTER LEAVING SAVANNAH at her door, Kit took a long walk on the beach and then a very long, very cold shower. Neither helped. He was still hard and aroused when he went to bed, still both frustrated and baffled by her behavior.

Maybe he would have tried to change her mind if he hadn't seen her expression when she'd asked him to stop. He could have seduced her with pretty words, with experienced touches and skilled caresses. And maybe he would have succeeded. But he wouldn't have been able to forget that she had asked him to stop with fear in her eyes.

The fear had shaken him. At first, he'd thought she was afraid of *him*. Afraid that he wouldn't take her rejection well. That he would try to overpower her, despite her resistance. And that had hurt. Surely the hours they'd spent together had taught her more about him than that.

He hadn't wanted to stop. But that didn't mean he was an animal, unable to control his impulses.

Sometime during his walk on the beach, he'd come to the conclusion that it hadn't been *his* reactions Savannah had feared. It had been her own.

He supposed he could understand that, to an extent. Because if he was totally truthful with himself, he'd have to admit that the powerful attraction between them scared the hell out of him, too.

He hadn't expected to fall this hard. This fast. And he wasn't entirely sure what he was going to do about it. He only knew that he wasn't ready to walk away from what he'd found during these past two days in paradise.

After a restless night, Kit slept late the next morning. He awoke somewhat rested, invigorated, and more determined than ever to convince Savannah that what was happening between them was unique. Special. Not something they could ignore, no matter how hard she might try.

He was aware of how foolishly he was behaving. He felt like an infatuated schoolboy as he shaved and dressed, taking extra pains with his appearance. When was the last time he'd acted like this about any woman? Ninth grade?

He didn't even know her last name.

But that, he told himself as he slipped on his shoes, was going to change. They'd spent yesterday just enjoying each other's company, indulging in a bit of fantasy. Today they were going to talk.

He had only three days left on the island. And he wanted to spend those days getting to know Savannah better.

She'd said she was from Georgia. He lived on the west coast. Could be a problem. Then again, he'd never been one to be bothered by minor details. Not when something mattered to him.

Three days from now, he would know whether Savannah fit permanently into that category.

It was another gorgeous day on Serendipity Island. As he strode purposefully toward Savannah's cottage, Kit wondered briefly if his old friend Rafe ever tired of waking up in paradise. Actually, Rafe seemed incredibly happy with his wife and his son and his thriving resort. Kit envied the contentment Rafe had found, something that had been sadly missing from his own life of late.

Kit noticed that the door to Savannah's cottage stood

open. Was she just letting in some fresh air? Security was tight at Rafe's resort, but still Kit was a bit surprised—anyone could walk in on her. Maybe she was from one of those small Southern towns where people still felt safe leaving their doors unlocked. Having spent the past few years dividing his time between New York and L.A., Kit wasn't so trusting.

He paused on the threshold. He could hear two women chattering in the bedroom. He couldn't hear them well enough to make out the words, but he didn't think they were speaking English.

Apparently, he'd caught the maids at work. Savannah must have already gone out. He wondered if she'd left a message for him. Or was she deliberately avoiding him after last night? Was she going to make it necessary for him to track her down and insist that they talk?

He stepped inside the living room. "Hello," he called out.

A dark-haired, dark-eyed maid in the white resort uniform appeared in Savannah's doorway, smiling.

"May I help you, sir?" the woman asked in intriguingly-accented English.

"I'm looking for Miss—er, for the woman who's staying in this cottage. Have you seen her this morning?"

The maid shook her head. "The lady checked out this morning, sir. She took the first launch off the island."

Kit couldn't believe it. "No, she couldn't have checked out."

Surely she hadn't been *that* shaken by what had happened—or rather, what had almost happened—between them.

"I'm sorry, sir. I saw her leave this morning."

"She must have been called away. Some sort of emergency at home, perhaps." He didn't want to believe that she'd run from him.

The maid glanced at a small notepad she wore clipped to her belt. "No, sir. The lady was scheduled to leave this morning. This was her original departure date."

Which meant Savannah had known last night, when he'd left her at her door, that she wouldn't be seeing him again. And she hadn't said a word.

Realizing that the maid was watching him closely, Kit forced a smile and nodded. "My mistake," he murmured. "I'm sorry I've disturbed your work."

"No problem. Have a nice day, sir."

His smile faded. He turned to leave, but paused in the doorway. The woman probably already thought he was nuts; another dumb question couldn't do any further harm. "I don't suppose you know her last name?"

The maid shook her head. "I'm afraid not. We always came in to clean when she was out. We never actually spoke to her. We referred to her only as the pretty lady in Number 12."

The pretty lady in Number 12. Kit realized that he knew little more about Savannah than this woman did.

Funny. He'd thought he'd gotten to know her rather well during the few days they'd spent together. Looked as if he'd been wrong. Because he certainly hadn't expected it to end like this.

SITTING ON AN AIRPLANE headed toward Atlanta, squeezed between two broad-shouldered businessmen, Savannah stared down into the open jewelry box she held in her hands. The flower-shaped pin Kit had given her glittered as if with a fresh coat of morning dew, looking as if it had just been plucked from an exotic vine.

She told herself that she would treasure the pin forever. Any time her life got too hectic or too lonely, she would be able to look at the brooch and remember a few perfect, magical hours. With memories like those, she couldn't possibly have regrets, she told herself as she blinked back a film of tears that she tried to attribute to weariness.

She wondered if Kit would remember her with fondness, or with anger because she'd left the way she did.

She wondered if Kit would remember her at all.

"TELL ME WHERE to find her." Kit's voice was firm. Commanding. Desperate. "I know you have her name and address in your files. Let me have them."

Rafe Dancer was not easily intimidated. He shook his head. "You know I can't do that. If she'd wanted you to have her address, she would have given it to you herself. I cannot violate the privacy of one of my guests."

"Damn it, Rafe, you know me. You know I won't harass her. I only want to find her and talk to her. If she asks me to get lost, I will. Let me have the address."

"No, Kit. Not even for you."

Hissing a curse, Kit whirled to pace Rafe's office with angry, frustrated strides.

Leaning against his desk, his arms crossed over his blindingly white shirt, Rafe watched his friend patiently. "What did you say to her to make her angry?"

"Nothing," Kit snapped. "She ran because she got cold feet. Because what started out as a holiday flirtation turned into a hell of a lot more."

"You knew her...what? A few days?"

"It doesn't matter. I have to find her. Rafe..."

"No, Kit."

Kit slammed his fist on a delicate, and very expensive-looking cherry table. Miraculously, it didn't crumble. Rafe only continued to watch him, apparently unconcerned about his office decor.

"Tell me this," Kit said, turning to face his friend with narrowed eyes. "What would you have done if someone tried to keep you from T.J.?"

"I'd have gone for his throat," Rafe replied evenly. He tilted his head back slightly, baring his own. "Want to take a chance at it?"

Kit considered it. "If I take you on, and I win, will you give me Savannah's address?"

"No."

Kit blew air sharply out of his nostrils and turned away. "Some friend you are."

A muscle clenched in Rafe's jaw. "There are some things I simply can't do. Even for a friend."

Kit had the grace to be ashamed of his tantrum.

"Sorry," he muttered. "I just can't stand back and let her go without at least trying to talk to her one more time."

"Then find her. But you'll have to do it without my help."

Kit nodded grimly. "Then that's what I'll do."

"Good luck."

"For what it's worth," Kit said from the open doorway, "I respect your integrity, Rafe. I always have."

"Thank you, Kit. Be sure and let Ms. McBride know that I guarded her privacy, will you?"

"Yeah, sure, I'll—" Kit froze for a moment, suddenly aware of what Rafe had done.

"Thank you."

His face hard, Rafe jerked his chin toward the door. "If you'll excuse me, I have a great deal of work to do. Come back to the island any time, Kit. You're always a welcome guest here."

Kit nodded. "Maybe I'll come back for my honeymoon," he said flippantly, and then slipped out the office door before he made a further fool out of himself.

McBride. Savannah McBride, from Georgia.

Kit would find her if he had to work his way through every McBride in the whole damned state.

SAVANNAH'S FAMILY was waiting to meet her when she deplaned in Atlanta.

Miranda was wearing too much makeup, Savannah thought immediately, wincing at the sight of her thirteen-year-old daughter's colorfully painted face. Miranda's twin, Michael, stood slightly behind the others, his expression indicating that something had displeased him. Probably something his sister had said, Savannah thought with a stifled sigh. Her children hadn't been getting along very well lately, and the few days they'd just spent with their sometimes difficult grandmother probably hadn't helped things between them.

Savannah's mother, Ernestine Pratt McBride, wore an expression similar to her grandson's. Savannah recognized that look immediately. Ernestine was doing all she could to look as though a few days with her grandchildren had utterly exhausted her, just to make Savannah feel guilty about taking a vacation on her own.

This time, it wasn't going to work. Savannah had *needed* the time away. Needed the rest, the peace, the temporary escape from stress. She'd needed the sheer fun she'd had with Kit, though he'd probably had no idea how much their time together had meant to her.

But she couldn't think about Kit now. Not if she didn't want her family to suspect something important had happened to her during the last few days—unfortunately, something that couldn't last.

She reached her children first, and opened her arms to them. Miranda rushed right up for a hug, chattering a mile a minute about everything that had happened to her while Savannah had been gone. Michael responded a bit more sedately, but his hug was tight enough to let Savannah know that he had missed her.

Ernestine unbent enough to kiss her daughter's cheek. "Your vacation must have been good for you," she acknowledged rather reluctantly. "Looks like you got some rest."

"I did. And it felt great. Now I'd like to treat you to a nice dinner to thank you for taking care of the kids for me."

Ernestine's expression brightened. "There's that new Italian place I've been wanting to try while we're here in Atlanta. The one where all the celebrities eat when they come to town."

Savannah thought of her travel-wrinkled clothes and severely dented bank account. She would have preferred to go straight home to Campbellville—nearly an hour's drive away—take a long, hot bath and fall face-first into bed. But she knew what it took to keep her mother happy. After all, she'd been doing it for so very long.

"All right, Mother. If that's where you'd like to eat, that's fine with me."

With only a slight pang, she pushed her tropical memories to the back of her mind, tucked the flower pin safely into her purse, and stepped back into her real life.

SAVANNAH HAD TO WORK on her birthday. She managed to smile as her co-workers at the construction company feted her with gifts and teasing remarks about turning thirty.

By the time she climbed out of her car in her garage that evening, she was exhausted from being gracious. She had decided that it was a lot less tiring to put in a full day's work than to spend eight hours celebrating a birthday.

But the celebration wasn't over. As soon as she opened the door to the house she shared with her children and her mother, she heard the twins sing out, "Happy birthday!"

Savannah pasted on her tired, birthday-girl smile and pushed wistful thoughts of a long, hot bath to the back of her mind. It would be a while yet before she could enjoy such solitary luxury.

Ernestine prepared dinner for Savannah's birthday celebration at home. Afterward, the twins cleaned the kitchen with a minimum of squabbling—a rare concession in honor of the occasion. And then they insisted that Savannah open her gifts.

Ernestine gave her daughter a collection of expensive, scented lotions and creams designed to hide the signs of aging. Knowing what was expected of her, Savannah acted suitably thrilled to receive the gift.

She fully expected to see the charge for the gift on her next credit-card statement. Savannah had provided the sole support for her mother and children since Ernestine—still several years from retirement age—had developed a lung infection two years ago and had since declared herself too delicate to return to work.

Savannah didn't mind supporting her mother, considering it more of a debt. Despite her outspoken disapproval and obvious humiliation, Ernestine had been there for Savannah when Savannah found herself expecting twins at a time when she was little more than a child herself.

Ernestine had sacrificed a great deal to make a new home for her daughter and her grandchildren in a town where they could live comfortably and quietly, supporting all of them until Savannah had been able to take over as the breadwinner. Ernestine still helped a great deal around the house, doing most of the cooking, shopping and cleaning, though not, of course, without occasionally pointing out everything she did. But there were times when the magnitude of Savannah's own responsibilities got to her, resulting in migraine headaches she felt compelled to hide, and a steady diet of antacid tablets.

Though Savannah loved her mother, Ernestine was not an easy woman to live with.

When the long day finally ended, Savannah hugged her daughter and son, then sent them off to bed. She felt a pang at how quickly they were growing. Miranda was as tall as Savannah now, a full five feet four inches. Michael was two inches taller. And they were only thirteen.

Where had her babies gone?

Savannah spent the rest of her birthday doing laundry and getting ready for the next day. By the time she went to bed—the last one in the household to do so, as usual—she felt tired and rather old.

Because her bedroom seemed unusually quiet and

lonely, she turned on her radio while she cleaned her face and applied the new night cream her mother had given her. The volume of the easy-listening channel was turned low, and she paid little attention to the tunes as she dressed for bed. She had only wanted something to fill the silence.

And then she recognized a melody and felt hot tears fill her eyes.

"Star Dust." The blatantly sentimental tune suddenly seemed to fill the room. If she closed her eyes and tried very, very hard, she could almost imagine that she was back on a beach in the moonlight, feeling young and happy and carefree as Kit swept her into his arms for a midnight dance.

She'd wanted memories, she reminded herself. She'd thought they would comfort her.

How could she have known that they would torment her, instead?

She wondered for at least the hundredth time since she'd returned from Serendipity if Kit—wherever he was—ever thought of her.

5

A GAGGLE of ladies greeted Savannah when she dragged herself home from work Thursday evening, almost two weeks after her vacation. She'd had to work late, and was so tired it was all she could do to summon a smile for her mother's hospital auxiliary club, who were having a dessert party in the living room.

The women descended on her the moment she walked in the door.

"Savannah. How nice to see you."

"Oh, dear, you look so tired. You're working too hard."

"Please join us, Savannah. There's plenty of food left."

Savannah would have loved to keep walking, straight to her room and her bed. She really didn't mind her mother entertaining her friends, and Savannah genuinely liked most of the women in the room, but she simply wasn't in the mood for a party this evening.

For some reason, she hadn't been feeling very energetic since she'd returned from her vacation. For a while, Ernestine had been concerned that Savannah had picked up a tropical illness on the island.

But Savannah knew exactly what she'd brought home from her vacation—memories that were proving to be more haunting that she'd expected, and dreams that tormented her with what-might-have-beens.

She'd reassured her mother that she wasn't ill—unless being lovesick counted. And that was one conversation Savannah *didn't* want to get into!

So, she held onto her forced smile and agreed to have a slice of Mrs. O'Leary's red-velvet cake. Not to be slighted, Mrs. Burleson immediately insisted that Savannah try a bite of her lemon cream puff, and Mrs. Avery slipped her a pecan-laden fudge brownie.

Ernestine brought her daughter a glass of iced tea. "Dick kept you working late tonight, didn't he?" she asked in a tone that expressed both disapproval and concern.

"I had paperwork to finish," Savannah explained, then swallowed a moan when she spotted Lucy Bettencourt bearing down on them.

Lucy was, without doubt, the most avid gossip in Campbellville. Nothing escaped her ears, and any details she didn't know, she was quite willing to make up. Not that anyone ever actually had the nerve to accuse her of lying, of course. Getting sideways with Lucy Bettencourt was a surefire way of ending up on her verbal hit list.

Savannah was always very careful to watch her back when Lucy was around.

"Savannah, darlin', what a lovely pantsuit. Did you get that at Sophie's?"

Savannah smiled and shook her head. "I picked it up the last time I was in Atlanta," she explained.

"Well, it just looks darlin' on you. Dark slacks are such a clever way to minimize the hips, aren't they?"

Savannah held onto her smile. "That's what they say."

"And where are those precious twins of yours this evening?"

"Miranda's spending the evening with her friend Jessica Helper. And Michael is sleeping in a tent in Nick Whitley's backyard. Nick's parents agreed to have a camp-out for a few of Nick's friends."

Mrs. Bettencourt nodded sagely. "That little Jessica Helper is a sweet child. Too bad she got her mama's crooked nose, but maybe she can have it fixed someday. I heard that Toni saved up enough to have hers done a few years back, but then Marv's business got into trouble and she had to use the money to bail him out. Such a shame."

Savannah refused to comment on the Helpers' financial woes. She didn't mind that Miranda and Jessica were such close friends since, with the exception of being a bit too fond of makeup and boys, Jessica was a good kid.

Michael's latest best friend, Nick, was a different story.

Nick wasn't exactly a bad boy—yet. But he had a predilection for mischief that worried Savannah, especially since Michael thought everything Nick did was extremely cool. Since entering junior high, Michael had changed from an easygoing, affectionate and eager-to-please child to a moody, reticent and occasionally rebellious teenager. While Savannah supposed she should have anticipated the transformation, she missed her sweet little boy. And she worried.

It wasn't easy raising a son in a houseful of women.

As if she'd followed Savannah's line of thinking, Mrs. Bettencourt clucked her tongue. "That Whitley boy worries me. He's got a mean streak. Just like his daddy at the same age. I declare, Ernie Whitley was a handful, on his way to becoming a juvenile delinquent until his grandpa finally took him in hand and straightened him out. That boy of Ernie's has the same look about him. You better watch your son if he's keeping close company with Nick."

Savannah could almost feel the blood trickling from the corner of her mouth as she bit her tongue to keep from telling Lucy to go jump into the nearest lake.

Ernestine spoke up quickly, giving Savannah a cautioning look. "We watch Michael very closely, Lucy. He's a good boy. Hasn't given us any trouble."

Lucy glanced sideways at Savannah and nodded. "I'm sure you're both proud of him. He and his sister are certainly nice-looking children. They look very much like you, Savannah. Except for the shape of their eyes. They must have gotten those round eyes from their father."

There was just a hint of a question in the statement. Lucy had been trying to find out who had fathered Savannah's twins ever since Ernestine and Savannah had moved to town. Since Campbellville was over two hours' drive from Honoria, no one here knew about Savannah's humiliation with the captain of the football team, and she intended to keep it that way.

Her twins had been told that their biological father had been Savannah's high-school boyfriend, that the relationship had ended with the pregnancy, and that their father had no interest in seeing them at this point—his loss, Savannah had always assured them fervently. She'd encouraged them to come to her if they had any questions, but warned them to keep their family business private. If their friends asked questions, she'd said, all they had to do was answer that their parents had separated before they were born and that they'd never known their father. And then change the subject.

Savannah followed the latter part of her own advice now. "How is Gareth, Lucy? I've heard that he is recovering remarkably well from his surgery last month."

The distraction worked, this time. Lucy immediately launched into a slice-by-slice description of her younger son's recent hernia operation.

One touchy subject successfully avoided, Savannah thought in relief. But she knew there would be others, particularly when she saw Lucy's best friend, Marie Butler, looking her way. Catching Savannah's eye, Marie sniffed and put her brightly dyed red head close to the woman beside her.

Marie was still annoyed with Savannah for rejecting her son, Eric, who'd pursued Savannah publicly and determinedly for over a year before finally conceding defeat. Eric was a nice enough guy, but Savannah simply hadn't been inclined to date him. He wasn't that fond of children, for one thing, and her kids hadn't particularly liked him. And her kids were her main priority.

It wasn't that Marie had been delighted with Savannah as a potential daughter-in-law. But it bothered her greatly that everyone in town knew Savannah had been the uninterested one, rather than Marie's precious Eric.

Savannah sent Marie a sweet smile and turned back to Mrs. Bettencourt.

It was going to be a long evening.

Longer than she realized.

TO SAVANNAH'S RELIEF, the party was just beginning to show signs of breaking up when Miranda came home.

With a wince, Savannah noted immediately that Miranda had been into the makeup again. Her daughter was painted up like a super-model-in-training, she thought with a shake of her head.

Savannah was quite sure that the members of Ernestine's club would later whisper about what a terrible mother Savannah was.

With admirable patience, Miranda submitted to being examined and teasingly interrogated by her grandmother's friends, though she gave her mother a look that begged for rescue. Savannah indulged the ladies for a moment, then slipped an arm around her daughter's shoulders and directed a smile at the room in general.

"If you ladies will excuse us, it's getting late. I'm going up with Miranda so she can tell me about her evening while she gets ready for bed. Good night."

A chorus of good-nights answered her. It was with a sense of relief that both Savannah and Miranda made their escape.

Miranda started chattering about the movie she'd seen almost before she and her mother left the living room. "It was so cool! The best 'Code' film yet."

"Cold film?" Savannah repeated quizzically, still thinking of a way to broach the subject of Miranda's overuse of cosmetics.

Miranda sighed gustily and turned to her mother. "Code," she said clearly. "Come on, Mom, you know what I'm talking about. It's the third film based on Christopher Pace's 'Code' books. Remember? *Code of Dishonor*? *Code of Silence*? *Code of Steel*? I *told* you that was what Jessica and I were seeing tonight."

Savannah nodded in apology. "Yes, I know you did. I remember now."

The film was rated PG-13, which had given Savannah a bit of concern until Miranda had pointed out that she was, in fact, thirteen. Besides, Miranda had reminded Savannah, Michael had already seen the film. And both of them had seen the previous two releases on video at a friend's house and they really weren't that bad. Just a little violent, she'd said earnestly. Maybe a little bad language. But nothing she hadn't already heard in school.

After being assured by Jessica's parents that the movie wasn't any worse than the usual cops-and-bad-guys film, and was actually much better written than most, Savannah had agreed to the outing.

"So you enjoyed the movie?" she asked, trying to pay more attention to her daughter as they headed up the stairs.

"It was great! Christopher Pace is, like, the best writer ever. His movies are funny and exciting and really cool. He's been on a whole bunch of TV shows lately—you know, promoting the film? And he's really good-looking. Jessica thinks he ought to star in his own films. She says he's even better than Chris O'Donnell. I think he's cute, and funny—he made Oprah laugh so hard her eyes watered—but he's sort of old. About your age, maybe."

"Thank you very much," Savannah said dryly.

Miranda giggled. "Oops. Sorry. I didn't mean you're old, of course."

"No, of course not."

"So, anyway..."

They had just reached the top of the stairs when the doorbell rang, interrupting Miranda's prattle.

Savannah looked behind her and sighed. "I'd better see who that is. I'll be right back."

She was aware that Miranda remained where she was, watching as Savannah hurried back down the stairs.

"Who is that?" Ernestine asked, standing in the living-room doorway.

"I don't know, yet, Mother," Savannah replied with forced patience. "Are you expecting anyone?"

"Not this late."

Savannah thought immediately of Michael, and fervently hoped that nothing had gone wrong with the backyard camp-out. She opened the door quickly.

The yellow porch light illuminated a face that had featured prominently in Savannah's fantasies for almost two weeks. For one stunned moment, she wondered if she was dreaming again.

"Kit?" Her voice came out in a whisper, hardly audible even to her own ears.

His dark eyes swept her face, and his expression was somehow both smug and uncertain, all at the same time.

"You forgot to say goodbye," he said in the deep, whisky-smooth voice that had murmured to her in her dreams.

Savannah couldn't quite believe that she wasn't imagining him—she'd missed him so very desperately. Without thinking, she reached out to touch his cheek.

He felt very real. Warm and solid, exactly the way she remembered him.

"I can't believe you're here," she murmured. She was unable to hide her pleasure at seeing him, and for one long, shimmering moment, everything else was forgotten.

His eyes locked with hers, Kit caught her hand and pressed a kiss against her palm. "I missed you," he said with devastating simplicity.

"Savannah?" Ernestine spoke impatiently from behind her. "Who is it?"

Savannah gasped and pulled her hand from Kit's, abruptly brought back to reality.

Kit was here! This man she'd met so briefly on vacation, this man whose last name she didn't even know, this man who was little more than a total stranger to her—with the exception of a few spectacular shared memories—had somehow followed her home. And now what in the world was she going to do with him?

Why was it that every time Savannah did something reckless and daring, it always came back to haunt her?

Kit looked at her apologetically. "I've obviously come at a bad time. You're entertaining."

"My mother's friends," she replied automatically. "They were just leaving. I can't believe you're here."

His expression turned rueful. "So you said."

Savannah realized that he was still standing on the front porch, that she was half in, half out the door, and that her mother and her daughter were hovering somewhere behind her, waiting to find out who had called at this hour. She hesitated for just a moment before inviting him in. She had the unsettling feeling that, once Kit stepped into her house, her life would never be the same.

SAVANNAH WASN'T exactly throwing herself into his arms in welcome.

Kit wanted to believe that it had been pleasure that had lit her face when she'd first recognized him standing at her door. When she'd reached out to touch him, he'd been sure that she was as glad to see him as he was to see her again. And then someone had spoken to her, and the fear he'd seen in her eyes that last night on the island had returned.

Why was Savannah so afraid of what she felt for him? And had he been wrong to follow his instincts and track her down?

She seemed to hesitate forever before finally stepping away from the door. "Please," she said, her tone a bit too stilted, a bit too polite. "Come in."

What he wanted to do was pull her into his arms and kiss her with all the hunger that had been building up during the two weeks they'd been apart. He'd tried to convince himself during that time that seeing her again would ease the urgency. Maybe, he'd told himself, he wouldn't even find her as attractive once they were away from the island.

He'd been wrong. He wanted her now as badly as he had that last night, when he'd reluctantly left her at her cottage door. And it was all he could do to keep from reaching out for her.

He held his hands firmly at his sides as he stepped past her into the modest frame house.

An older woman with suspicious blue eyes and hair-spray-stiffened frosted curls stood behind Savannah. Studying Kit curiously, a young teenage girl was descending the steps, a blond ponytail bouncing behind her, a bit too much color artificially added to her pretty face. The resemblance between Savannah and these two made Kit suspect a family connection.

Savannah confirmed his guess. "Mother," she said. "This is my friend, Kit. Er..."

She glanced quickly at him, silently reminding him that he hadn't yet told her his last name. And it struck him anew what a novelty it was to meet a beautiful woman who wasn't drawn to his fame or fortune.

"Kit Pace," he interjected smoothly, turning his most charming smile toward Savannah's mother.

She wasn't visibly enthralled. "Ernestine McBride," she said with a slight nod. "You aren't from around here, are you?"

"No," he admitted. "This is my first time in your area."

Kit noticed that several other middle-aged women had gathered close to the open archway leading into the living room, eyeing him with surreptitious curiosity. All of them looked as though they'd never seen a stranger before, he thought in discomfort. Didn't anyone in this little burg ever have visitors?

He really should have called, he thought belatedly. Savannah was obviously stunned by his appearance, and her mother didn't seem particularly pleased that her party had been interrupted. Kit couldn't help thinking of his own mother's frequent warnings that his habitual impulsiveness was going to get him in trouble someday.

The teenager Kit had noticed on the stairs suddenly gasped loudly, causing them all to look her way.

Kit found her standing very close to him, staring at him with wide, shocked blue eyes. She looked very much like Savannah, he mused. A much younger sister, perhaps? He supposed Ernestine McBride could have had a late-in-life baby.

"Oh, my g-gosh!" the girl stammered, her voice squeaking. "Do you know who you are?"

Since it wasn't the first time he'd been asked that odd question by someone who recognized him, Kit merely nodded and murmured, "Why, yes, I do."

And I really should have told Savannah before now, he thought when Savannah turned to the girl in startled question.

"What are you talking about, Miranda?" she asked.

"Oh, come on, Mom, you have to know who he is," Miranda breathed, almost vibrating with excitement. "He's Christopher Pace!"

Mom?

Kit stared at Savannah, wondering if he'd misunderstood, but somehow knowing that he hadn't. This was Savannah's daughter. And, oh, hell, he hoped she didn't have a husband lurking in some other room of the house!

Savannah was staring back at Kit with an answering shock in her eyes. While she might not have recognized his face, she apparently knew his name—and was utterly flabbergasted by learning the truth of his identity.

Ernestine—the girl's grandmother, Kit now realized—looked from Savannah to Miranda with a frown. "*Who* did you say?" she asked Miranda.

"He's Christopher Pace. The novelist and Hollywood screenwriter. The guy who wrote all the 'Code' books and the three 'Code' movies. Oh, man, I can't believe this! I just got home from seeing your latest movie. It was the best yet," the girl told Kit with awestruck enthusiasm.

By now, everyone in the living room had gathered in the doorway to stare at Kit. And he was wishing a very large hole would open in the floor and swallow him up.

He felt Savannah's gaze riveted to his face as he forced a smile for her daughter. *Her daughter. Oh, hell.*

"Thank you," he said.

He heard the buzz of excited whispers begin just as the doorbell chimed.

Since everyone else seemed to be too busy gawking at him to pay attention to the buzzer, Kit was beginning to wonder if *he* was going to have to get the door. Savannah finally moved, taking care not to brush against Kit as she passed him. Kit turned his head to watch her, sending her yet another silent message of apology that she couldn't seem to hear.

She opened the door to reveal a uniformed police officer standing on the doorstep, a sullen-looking teenage boy at his side.

"Sorry to bother you, Miz McBride, but we need to have a little talk," the officer drawled.

Savannah looked immediately at the boy—who, Kit couldn't help noticing with a sinking feeling, looked enough like Miranda to be her twin brother.

"Oh, Michael," Savannah groaned. "What have you done?"

Kit had thought to surprise Savannah by showing up unannounced on her doorstep.

He'd had no idea how many surprises had been in store for *him*.

SAVANNAH WAS AFRAID to even wonder what else could happen to her that evening. She was still trying to deal with her shock at finding Kit—*Christopher Pace!*—on her doorstep. And now Michael had been officially escorted home from what was supposed to have been an innocent backyard camp-out.

The ladies of the gossip club were going to have a field day tomorrow, she thought, painfully aware of the many curious eyes watching her.

She could only deal with one crisis at a time. She

glanced pleadingly at her mother, who immediately ushered her guests back into the living room. To Savannah's mingled relief and dismay, Kit and Miranda followed the others, leaving Savannah alone with her son and Officer Henshaw.

"What happened?" she demanded.

Michael didn't volunteer any information.

"Your boy was caught pushing over mailboxes on Bishop Road with a group of other kids," the officer said. "We've explained to him that vandalism is a serious offense, and that he could also be charged with trespassing, criminal mischief and interfering with the mail. Which, of course, is a federal offense," he added in a stern voice for the boy's benefit.

"Bishop Road?" Savannah frowned at her son. "That's on the other side of town. What in the world were you doing there when you knew you weren't supposed to leave Nick Whitley's yard?"

Michael shrugged. "All the guys were doing it. What was I supposed to do, sit in the backyard by myself?"

"You should have called me to come get you," Savannah informed him sharply.

Henshaw looked at Savannah. "I've already had a long talk with him about how much trouble he can get into by just going along with the crowd. He knows we could have taken the whole group of them down to the station and booked them. Chief Powell and I are giving them one more chance, but if they get into trouble again, they're going to have to deal with a juvenile-court judge."

Savannah knew that Henshaw was doing his best to scare Michael straight. She hoped it worked, and she certainly intended to do her part to make sure nothing like this ever happened again.

"By the time he's no longer grounded for this incident, he may no longer *be* a juvenile," she muttered, her gaze locked with Michael's.

Officer Henshaw fought a smile. "Sorry again that I had to interrupt your party, Miz McBride. Michael, you need to apologize to your mama and your grandmama for embarrassing them like this, you hear? And don't make me have to haul you home like this again, boy."

Michael shook his head. "No, sir."

Savannah wished her son had sounded just a bit more penitent. She still couldn't believe he'd done this. It was the first time he'd ever deliberately disobeyed her.

As soon as she had closed the door behind Officer Henshaw, Savannah turned to Michael, who was watching her warily.

"Go to your room," she said in a low voice that brooked no argument. "I'll deal with you as soon as your grandmother's guests have gone."

"But all my stuff is still over at Nick's."

"And it will stay there until tomorrow," she replied flatly. "Go to your room, Michael. Now."

He turned on one sneaker and headed for the stairs.

Savannah had to take a deep breath for composure before she walked into the living room. She immediately spotted Kit sitting on the sofa, easily charming an entire roomful of women who looked utterly delighted that a Hollywood celebrity had favored them with his presence.

So he hadn't been a hallucination, after all, Savannah thought dazedly. He really was here.

How on earth had he found her? And, more importantly, *why?*

"Is everything all right, Savannah dear?" Lucy Bettencourt asked, her tone sweet, her eyes too eager.

Savannah forced a smile. "Yes, everything's fine, thank you. I'm afraid Michael and his friends got into some mischief, but it's all been taken care of."

Lucy shook her head and clucked her tongue. "I warned you about that Nick Whitley," she murmured. "The boy is headed for trouble, and you don't want him taking your son with him."

Several of her friends gravely nodded agreement. Others looked embarrassed for Savannah's sake. Mildred Peeples, who happened to be Nick Whitley's great-aunt, looked torn between being worried and taking offense.

Barbara Mitchell, one of Savannah's favorite neighbors, swiftly changed the subject.

"Mr. Pace was just telling us how the two of you met on your vacation," Barbara said, with a quick smile at Kit.

To Savannah, it seemed that every expression in the room turned speculative. She knew people had thought it odd that she'd taken off for a Caribbean island by herself, leaving her family at home. They simply hadn't understood that she'd desperately needed to be entirely on her own for the first time in...well, ever.

"I explained that you'd invited me to Campbellville for my research on small Southern towns," Kit said quickly, and Savannah wondered if anyone in the room suspected that he was lying through his pretty white teeth.

"Can you imagine? Our little Campbellville as the setting for a bestseller." Annalee Grimes shook her bluish-gray head in amazement. "Wouldn't that be something?"

Kit smiled. "I wouldn't actually use Campbellville, of course," he corrected. "My books are a series about law enforcement officers in a not-too-distant future, battling futuristic criminals. I thought it would be interesting to create a futuristic Deep South. I'm just here to soak up some atmosphere."

The ladies listened intently to his explanation, some looking a bit bewildered, most fascinated.

Ernestine glanced from Savannah to Kit, then pointedly at her watch. "Goodness," she said rather loudly, "it's getting late, isn't it?"

Barbara Mitchell promptly rose from her seat. "It certainly is. We'd better be going."

Lucy Bettencourt showed a tendency to want to linger. Barbara didn't give her a chance. Within ten minutes, she had purses distributed, empty dessert dishes back to their rightful owners, and the ladies of the auxiliary on their way out the door. *Bless her heart,* Savannah thought fervently. She was definitely sending flowers to Barbara at the earliest opportunity.

The last guest finally departed, leaving only family—and Kit—in the McBride house. Savannah noted that Miranda was staring at Kit as if she were waiting for him to grow a second head.

Ernestine did not look pleased.

"What in the world," she demanded, "was Michael doing, to be brought home by the police?"

"We'll discuss that later," Savannah answered calmly. "Mother, Miranda, could you give me a moment to speak privately with my guest, please?"

"Oh, man. I can't believe you know Christopher Pace." Miranda turned her dazed eyes onto her mother. "Michael's going to go crazy. Why didn't you tell us?"

Avoiding Kit's eyes, Savannah motioned for her daughter to leave the room. "Go wash your face," she said. "It's almost bedtime."

Miranda seemed tempted to argue, looking longingly at Kit, but must have sensed from her mother's voice that this was not the time. Reluctantly, she left the room.

"Michael's upstairs, Mother," Savannah added to Ernestine. "Maybe you should have him tell you what he did tonight."

Having to confess to his socially conscious grandmother would be almost as serious a punishment as the grounding Savannah planned for him, she knew. Michael would hear the old lecture about not embarrassing the family, about guarding his reputation in the community, about taking pride in his good name. Heaven only knew Savannah had heard *that* talk often enough while growing up—not that it had stopped *her* from humiliating her mother, she thought grimly.

Was she now in danger of doing so again?

6

SAVANNAH WAITED until she'd heard her mother climb the stairs behind Miranda before turning to Kit. "What in the world are you doing here?"

"Before I answer that," he said, advancing purposefully toward her, "there's something I simply have to find out."

She didn't even have a chance to ward him off. Almost before she realized what he intended, he had her in his arms, her mouth crushed beneath his. And there was absolutely nothing she could do except lock her arms around his neck and lose herself in his kiss.

She had never expected that she would have the chance to kiss him again.

This time, though, they weren't standing on a windswept beach beneath a canopy of stars, in the pale light of a full moon. They were standing in Savannah's party-littered living room, under the same roof as Savannah's curious mother and children.

It didn't matter. This embrace was as powerful, as staggering, as electrifying as the ones they'd shared on Serendipity. Maybe even more so because it had been two weeks since they'd been together.

She'd been kidding herself by trying to believe that she and Kit had shared a pleasant vacation flirtation, something she could easily put behind her. Even if Kit hadn't shown up on her doorstep, she would never have forgotten him. Would never have stopped wondering about him, wishing she could be with him again.

She had considered a relationship between them impossible even before she'd known his full name. So impossible that she'd run away from him rather than take a chance at making a fool of herself again, at being hurt again. Now that he'd found her, and she'd discovered that he was a famous novelist, a celebrated screenwriter, a media favorite...well, that made it all the more terrifying that she had recklessly fallen for him.

He finally released her mouth and lifted his head with a look of satisfaction.

"That answered one question," he murmured, his voice husky.

"What question?" Her own voice was hoarse.

He drew a deep, slightly ragged breath. "One of my own. Now. Tell me why you left without saying goodbye."

Savannah winced in response to Kit's tone. She'd thought maybe he would be annoyed that she'd left the way she did, but it had never occurred to her that he'd be hurt.

"I didn't think a goodbye was...necessary," she answered awkwardly.

Kit frowned. "Necessary? No. But maybe it would have been polite?"

She doubted that he'd gone to all this trouble just to lecture her on her manners. "I'm sorry," she said, anyway. "I just didn't know what to say."

"You could have said that you had to leave, but that you'd had a nice time with me."

"I had a wonderful time with you," she admitted. "But—"

"You could have said you were really sorry we didn't have more time to get to know each other better."

"Well, yes, of course I would have enjoyed spending more time with you, but—"

"You could have given me your number, so that I could call you without tracking you down through the Internet. Unless, of course, you didn't want me to have your number. If that was the case, all you had to do was say you weren't interested. I'd have understood that."

He paused for a moment, then stunned her by adding, "I couldn't stop thinking about you, Savannah."

She moistened her lips, stalling while she tried to think of something to say. She could almost believe that she was imagining this entire conversation. It sounded eerily like the ones she'd been having in her dreams for the past two weeks.

After a taut moment of silence, Kit cleared his throat. "Um—Savannah? You want to give me a hint about what you're thinking? I don't know if you're glad to see me, or if you're hoping I'll disappear in a puff of smoke."

She looked up to find him standing quite close to her now, his smile rueful. Their gazes locked, and for just a moment she was transported back to the island, back to the fantasy. There was only Savannah and Kit, two people with nothing more on their minds than their next moonlit dance.

Just as she opened her mouth to assure him that she did not want him to disappear in a puff of smoke—or, if he did, that she would love to disappear with him for a while—she was interrupted. Her son burst inelegantly into the room, a paperback book in his hand and a wild look in his eyes. Apparently, his sister had been to visit him.

"You're Christopher Pace!" Michael almost shouted at Kit, waving the book frantically.

"Yes, I know," Kit answered mildly, turning from Savannah after only a slight hesitation. "And what's your name?"

"I'm Michael. Michael McBride."

The boy's face was flushed, his hair tumbling haphazardly over his forehead. Savannah hadn't seen her son looking so flustered since—well, ever, she thought ruefully.

Kit held out his hand. "Nice to meet you, Michael."

Michael shook Kit's hand almost reverently, then blurted, "What are you doing here?"

"Michael." Savannah shook her head in response to his lack of manners. She didn't want him to forget that he was still in serious trouble, but she wouldn't embarrass him further in front of his hero, she decided. She and her son would have their talk after Kit left.

"I'm a new friend of your mom's. I just stopped in to say hello while I was in the area."

"Oh, man. You're, like, my favorite writer ever. I just finished reading *Code of Thieves.* It was great."

"Thank you. It's always nice to meet someone who enjoys my books."

"So, could you, like, sign it for me or something?"

Kit promptly reached inside his jacket and pulled out a pen. "I'd be glad to."

"Oh, man." Michael looked delirious with pleasure.

Kit scribbled something in the book, signed his name with a flourish and handed it to Michael, who thanked him fervently.

"You're welcome," Kit replied. "It's been very nice

to meet you, Michael. I know your mother must be very proud of you."

Michael flushed, glanced quickly at his mother, then down at his feet, and mumbled something unintelligible.

"Yes," Savannah said firmly, "I'm very proud of both my children. They're good kids. They just need to learn to choose their friends a bit more carefully."

Michael's gulp was audible.

Kit shook his head and chuckled. "The worst trouble I ever got into was when I let a guy who was supposed to be my best friend talk me into doing something stupid. Nearly got us both killed. After we were rescued, I thought my dad was going to finish the job. Fortunately, he just grounded me for a month and made me work my punishment off in his hardware shop."

Michael looked up at Kit through his lashes. "That really happened?"

Kit nodded sympathetically. "Sure did. I knew it was a dumb thing to do, but I didn't want my friends to think I was chicken. I learned my lesson that time, though. Haven't you noticed that in my books, I often have basically decent guys go bad because they haven't learned to stand up for what they know is right when they're pressured to do something wrong?"

Michael nodded slowly. "Like Deke Irons in *Code of Vengeance.*"

"Exactly." Kit looked pleased that the boy had taken his point.

Michael looked thoughtful for a moment, then glanced at his mother again before turning back to Kit. "You were grounded for a whole month?"

Kit nodded gravely. "I didn't like it, of course, but even then I knew it was better than being in juvenile detention. Or dead," he added. "Remind me sometime, and I'll tell you the whole story. When I'm finished, you'll probably agree that I really got off easier than I deserved."

"I'd like to hear it," Michael agreed eagerly.

"Not tonight," Savannah said, deciding it was time to intercede. "It's getting late, Michael. Go back upstairs and get ready for bed. I'll be up soon."

Like his sister, Michael knew when arguing would get him nowhere. He probably realized he'd pressed his luck as far as it would go. He shook Kit's hand, said he hoped to see him again soon, and left the room, looking back over his shoulder until he was out of sight.

"What *did* you let your friend talk you into?" Savannah asked Kit curiously.

His smile was sheepish. "Playing chicken with a freight train. My shoe got caught under the rail. If I hadn't been able to get out of my sneaker at the last minute, I'd have been killed."

"Oh, my God." Savannah wished now that she hadn't asked. The thought of her son doing anything that stupid was enough to make her want to lock him in his room until he turned thirty.

"You look pretty much the way my mom did when she found out what I'd done," Kit said ruefully. "She didn't have to say a word to make me feel like a real jerk. She let one little tear trickle down her cheek, and I threw myself at her feet and cried and promised her I'd never do anything like that again."

Savannah laughed shakily and ran a weary hand through her hair. "You think that would work for me and Michael?"

Kit rubbed his jaw thoughtfully. "A little mother-guilt never hurts," he said after a moment. "But my dad's tough punishment was pretty darn effective, too."

"Then I'll have to find a way to combine the two, since I've had to fill both roles since the twins were born."

"You're—er—divorced?"

She'd told him on the island that she'd never been married. Either he'd forgotten, or he was trying to be tactful. Savannah shook her head. "I wasn't married to their father. He never claimed responsibility for them."

She figured he might as well understand completely that the lighthearted woman he'd met on the island who'd been free to dance and play and flirt with attractive strangers, the woman he'd come looking for, didn't exist. She doubted that he would have been as likely to follow her had he known she was a single mother of twin teenagers, solely responsible for them and their grandmother.

Kit slipped his hands into the pockets of his slacks. "You didn't tell me you had children."

"There were a lot of things I didn't tell you," she reminded him.

"Why?"

She shook her head, wondering how she could make him understand. "Because it wasn't real. It was like a...like a fantasy," she said inadequately. "A tropical island, an attractive man, romantic music. I knew our lives were nothing alike, but for those few hours it didn't matter."

He looked momentarily confused. "So you knew all along that I was Christopher Pace?"

"No. Not until Miranda let it slip tonight. I told you, I don't follow celebrity news much. I didn't know."

"Then what made you think our lives were so different?"

"Just a feeling, I guess," she admitted. "But, obviously, I was right. You've caught a glimpse of my life tonight, Kit. I have my kids to look after. And my mother. There's very little time for fun and adventure. In fact, this was probably the most exciting party my mother's friends have ever attended. They'll talk about it for weeks."

"And you hate that." His dark eyes were focused intently on her face, seeing more than she'd expected.

She nodded. "I don't like providing grist for the gossip mills. I've been in that position enough to know that it can get ugly."

"Trust me, gossip is something I know all too well."

She almost shuddered at the thought of how Kit's life, like many celebrities, was open to discussion and speculation by anyone with an access to the media, no matter how sleazy or disreputable the source might be. She had often thought that she was glad she'd outgrown her girlhood dreams of fame and fortune, since she would truly hate living her life in a public fishbowl. She couldn't help wondering if Kit's appearance in Campbellville was going to thrust her into it, whether she liked it or not.

But even with that fear at the back of her mind, she couldn't honestly say she was sorry Kit was there.

"Oh, Kit," she murmured, stress and exhaustion loosening her tongue. "Why did you have to come here? It was so much safer when you were just a fantasy."

He was standing close enough to her now to reach out and touch her cheek. "I already told you why I'm here. I couldn't stop thinking about you."

He slid his fingertips along the line of her jaw, making her shiver. "I wanted to see you. Touch you. Dance with you again."

Savannah was trembling now, her hands itching to slide around his neck and into the soft thickness of his luxurious dark hair. He had only to speak in that low, sexy voice to take her back to the fantasy, she realized numbly. She could almost hear sultry music begin to play in the background.

"You don't even know me," she reminded him in a whisper.

"I know enough to want to know more. Are you going to give me that chance, Savannah, or are you going to send me away?"

She searched his face with questioning eyes. Was he really still interested in her? Didn't he understand how difficult—if not downright impossible—a relationship between them would be? "And if I ask you to leave?"

"I'll go," he answered promptly. And then gave her that pirate's smile she hadn't been able to resist on the island. "But not without trying to change your mind."

With that warning, he lowered his mouth to hers again. And if Kit had any second thoughts about having come looking for her, she certainly couldn't tell from his kiss. He kissed her as heatedly, as eagerly as he had on the island, when the magic between them had taken them both by surprise. And this kiss, like the last one, might have flared into mutual passion had not a gasp from the doorway broken them apart as effectively as a pail of cold water.

Savannah jerked out of Kit's arms, then cursed herself for reacting to the interruption as if she was still a teenager, caught doing something she shouldn't. Savannah glanced at her mother, who was looking quickly from Savannah to Kit, her expression a combination of surprise and disapproval.

"I'll walk Kit out," Savannah said with hard-won composure. "And then I really must go upstairs and talk to Michael."

"Good night, Mrs. McBride." Kit flashed Ernestine another of his winning smiles. Had it been directed at Savannah, her knees might have buckled.

If Ernestine had any reaction at all, she concealed it well. She merely nodded. "Good night, Mr. Pace."

"I don't think your mother will be joining the Christopher Pace fan club any time soon," Kit murmured to Savannah as they stood at her open front door.

Savannah shrugged. "Mother tends to be suspicious of strangers."

"And so does Savannah, I think," Kit observed, watching her expression.

Savannah grimaced. "Maybe a little," she agreed.

"I'm not a threat to you, Savannah. I didn't look you up to hurt you or embarrass you, though it probably didn't seem that way this evening. I only wanted to spend more time with you. I said it earlier, and I'll repeat it—if you want me to disappear, just say so."

She knew she should ask him to go away. There was no way anything permanent could happen between them. And she wasn't interested in a fling. Even if she didn't care about her own reputation, she had her children to consider.

But she didn't want him to go. She hadn't been able to stop thinking about him since he'd left her at the door of her cottage. Now that he was here with her again, she didn't have the willpower to send him away.

"I don't want you to disappear, Kit. But—"

He smiled and covered her mouth with his fingertips. "That's all I wanted to hear. I'll see you tomorrow."

She sighed faintly and nodded. "I can meet you for lunch, if you'd like," she said from behind his muffling fingers.

He removed his hand to brush his mouth across hers. "Fine. I'll call you in the morning to set something up."

"Call early. I leave for work at 7:45."

"Then I'll call at 7:30," he said, apparently undaunted by the early hour.

"Don't you need my number?"

His pirate smile flashed in the dim light. "I already have it."

Of course he did.

"You," Savannah told him, "are dangerous."

"Not to you," he promised. "Good night, Savannah. This time, I really will see you tomorrow, yes?"

She managed not to wince at the little dig. "Yes."

He kissed her briefly, but thoroughly enough to make her heart pound in her chest. And then he turned and sauntered away.

He whistled the tune to "Star Dust" as he walked toward his car, and she knew he'd chosen that particular song as a deliberate reminder of their magical evening on the beach. As if she needed reminding, she thought as she closed the door behind him.

"What," Ernestine asked from behind her, "was that all about?"

Savannah drew a deep breath and turned. "As Kit has already explained, I met him while I was on vacation. He wanted to see me again."

"I knew it was a bad idea for you to go off to that island by yourself," Ernestine muttered. "Now you've gone and gotten involved with some slick Hollywood type who'll break your heart and make us the talk of the town."

Savannah was tempted to argue, even though she was aware that there might be a grain of truth in her mother's pessimistic prediction. But for now, she had other things to attend to.

"I have to go up and talk to Michael now, Mother. Good night—and try not to worry about Kit, all right?"

Savannah would do enough worrying for both of them.

"Don't try to tell me he's only here for research," Ernestine called out as Savannah climbed the stairs. "I saw him kissing you."

"I'm not trying to tell you anything, Mother," Savannah said quietly over her shoulder. "Good night."

Ernestine was still muttering when Savannah reached the top of the stairs and turned down the hallway toward her son's room.

MICHAEL SAT cross-legged in the middle of his bed, gazing reverently at the paperback novel in his hands. His twin sat beside him, looking at the book as if expecting it to sprout wings and fly around the room.

Honestly, Savannah thought, taking in the scene, who would have imagined her children would be so starstruck?

"I can't believe you didn't tell us you know Christopher Pace," Miranda breathed, staring at her mother as though seeing her for the first time.

"I only spent a few hours with him and I wasn't sure I'd ever see him again," Savannah explained honestly. "I didn't see any real need to mention it."

Michael rolled his eyes. "You didn't see the need to mention that you met *the* Christopher Pace?"

Savannah decided not to explain that she hadn't known Kit was "*the* Christopher Pace" until Miranda had told her. She certainly didn't want her very bright children to even suspect that she had come heart-stoppingly close to having a vacation affair with a man whose last name she hadn't even known.

"I—er—guess I didn't quite realize how famous he is," she said lamely, instead.

"Mom, he won an Academy Award for the screen-play of his last movie," Miranda protested. "How could you not know that? Don't you even read the newspapers?"

"When I have time. And then only the news section. Not the gossip," Savannah answered evenly, though she was shaken by this new piece of information about the man who'd tracked her down because he claimed that he couldn't stop thinking of her.

"But the Academy Awards are news, not gossip," Miranda argued. "Gossip would be all those articles about the beautiful movie stars he's always dating."

Savannah didn't quite flinch, but she felt her stom-ach drop. "Get ready for bed, Miranda," she said, just a bit more sharply than she'd intended. "I need to talk to your brother."

Dragging her feet every step of the way, Miranda left the room.

"I know what I did was wrong," Michael said the minute Miranda closed the door behind her. "And I won't ever do it again, I promise."

Savannah knew full well that he had just said exactly what he thought she wanted to hear. Again, she was concerned by the lack of true penitence in his tone.

"What were you doing on Bishop Road when you were supposed to be at Nick's house? And how did you get there?"

"We rode bikes. I borrowed Nick's, and he rode his dad's. His dad said it was okay if we rode around town for a while. He said we couldn't have much fun just sitting in a tent, so we met Russell and Jeremy over at the Freemans', and then we went down Bishop Road."

"And whose bright idea was it to knock over mailboxes along the way?"

Michael shrugged. "I dunno. One of the guys did it and then everybody started doing it. It wasn't any big deal, really. We didn't tear them up or anything. All they have to do is put 'em back in the holes."

"Michael, vandalism is a *very* big deal. And so is interfering with the mail. That's a federal offense! Didn't you hear a thing Officer Henshaw said?"

"Nick's dad said Henshaw was making a big fuss over nothing. He said that we were just being kids and having a little fun, and he didn't see what was all that bad about it."

Savannah was appalled. "Nick's father said all of that in front of you?"

Michael nodded. "They called him to come get the bikes. He told Henshaw off pretty good."

Savannah planted her fists on her hips.

"You will call him *Officer* Henshaw, is that clear? He is an officer of the law and you will speak to him and about him with respect. As far as Nick's father is concerned, if he chooses to raise his boy to be a criminal, that's between him and the police department. But you will follow *my* rules when you are out of my sight. Have you got that straight?"

Michael shrugged.

"I want an answer, Michael. Now."

"Yes, ma'am," he mumbled.

"Good. And you'd better mean it, because I'm dead serious. As of tonight, you're grounded. For two weeks. You may go to baseball practice and to games, to church and to your Scout meetings. There will be no parties, no hanging out at the mall with your friends, no sleepovers, no phone calls. And you can't have your friends over here, either."

"But, Mom—"

She forged on. "If there is any monetary damage from this episode, it comes out of your allowance. Now, have I convinced you that this was, indeed, a 'big deal' and that it had better not happen again?"

Her son nodded sullenly. "I bet none of the other guys get grounded," he muttered.

"Well, I'm not their mother, am I?" Savannah retorted, then almost winced at hearing her own mother's words tumbling out of her mouth. She had always hoped to avoid those tired old parenting clichés with her children, but sometimes they just escaped of their own volition, it seemed.

"I'm punishing you as much for your attitude now as for what you did tonight. We'll be talking more about this, Michael, but now I'm tired and angry and I think it's best if we both calm down before we discuss it any further. Good night."

"'Night." His answer was barely audible.

By the time Savannah was finally able to close herself into her own bedroom that evening, she was a nervous wreck. This day had simply been too much to handle, she thought with a weary shake of her head. She felt as though she was balanced on a wire with her family's entire future on her shoulders, and adding just one more element would make it all come crashing down.

She sincerely hoped that Kit wouldn't prove to be that one disastrous element.

THE CAMPBELLVILLE grapevine was amazingly efficient. The moment Savannah walked into her office the next morning, she knew the gossip lines had already been activated.

A cluster of co-workers gathered in one corner of the main room stopped talking abruptly when Savannah entered. Someone cleared his throat. Someone else coughed. The group broke up quickly, though Savannah was aware of the surreptitious glances thrown her way.

From the reception desk, outspoken Patty Grant was the first to greet her. "Is what I heard true?" she demanded.

Savannah swallowed a groan. "I don't know, Patty. What did you hear?"

"I saw Annalee Grimes when I stopped at the doughnut shop on my way to work this morning. Annalee said she was at your house last night when Christopher Pace showed up on your doorstep. *The* Christopher Pace!"

"Then, yes, what you heard is true. I met Kit while I was on vacation. He was talking about setting his next book in the South and I suggested that he use Campbellville as research." The lie Kit had concocted slipped a bit too easily from her own tongue, she thought guiltily.

Patty's eyes widened. "He's going to put Campbellville in a book?"

Since Savannah was already committed to the excuse Kit had provided—which, she had to admit, was much more innocuous than the real reason he'd given for tracking her down—she answered firmly. "No. He's going to create a fictional small Southern town of the future. He just wanted to study the atmosphere here to give his setting a realistic feeling."

"Wow. Why didn't you tell us you knew Christopher Pace?"

Savannah grimaced. "Maybe I didn't think anyone would believe me," she suggested, trying to smile.

"I'd have believed you," Patty insisted. "Well...I might have thought you were teasing at first, but I would have believed you if you'd sworn it was true. I'd love to hear all the details about how you met him and what you talked about and everything. Is he really as good looking as he is on TV?"

"He's very attractive," Savannah answered vaguely. "Excuse me, Patty, I have some calls I have to make before nine o'clock."

Patty wasn't pleased to have the fascinating conversation cut short, but she didn't try to detain her supervisor any longer.

By the time she was supposed to leave for lunch, Savannah wished heartily that she'd called in sick that morning. One more speculative look, one more sympathetic approach about her "problems" with her son, one more avid question about Christopher Pace, and she would be tempted to scream, she thought in exasperation. Her staff could hardly concentrate on their jobs for prying into her personal life.

Something told her that her relatively anonymous life in Campbellville would never be the same....

7

KIT FELT RIDICULOUS as he waited for Savannah in a booth in the very back of a small diner some ten miles out of Campbellville. Savannah had been so furtive when she set up this meeting, he wouldn't have been entirely surprised if she'd asked him to wear a disguise.

Why was she so afraid to be seen with him? It wasn't as if no one knew he was in town. He would bet the women who'd met him last night had already spread the news throughout the county, judging by their unabashed questions about why he was there and how long he planned to stay.

He was accustomed to the curiosity and attention. Savannah apparently wasn't.

He wondered how much of it she would be willing to endure for them to spend more time together.

He'd been waiting approximately ten minutes when she finally appeared. She headed straight for the horseshoe-shaped back booth where she'd told him to wait. She wore a cream-colored short-sleeved sweater with navy slacks, and her hair was pulled into a neat twist at the back of her head. She looked as though she were going to a PTA meeting. She had obviously dressed so as not to draw attention to herself.

Kit could have told her it wasn't working. Savannah McBride was a woman who would be noticed whatever she was wearing. Men would admire her, women envy her, but they would both most definitely notice her.

She slid into the booth beside him with little more than a nod of greeting. "I'm sorry I'm late. I had an errand to run on my way."

Kit searched her face. "You're angry."

She grimaced. "Yes."

"At me?" Kit wondered if she was annoyed that he had tracked her down. He supposed he couldn't blame her if she was, but he hoped he could convince her that he had only wanted to see her again.

But Savannah shook her head. "I just picked up my son's things from the house of the friend he was supposed to stay with last night. The other boy's father ridiculed me for grounding Michael. He made a point of making fun of me in front of his son, who is not being punished at all."

Kit shook his head. "He's not doing his son any favors if he lets him get away with breaking the law."

She let out a sharp breath. "Are you kidding? He was practically patting him on the back in pride. He thought the entire incident was funny. The kind of thing teenage boys naturally do when they get together."

"I can concede that young boys—and girls, for that matter—tend to get into mischief when they're left unsupervised," Kit murmured. "But that doesn't mean they should be encouraged. They have to learn responsibility and self-control, and to understand the consequences of their actions. I think it's the job of the parents to teach those lessons before the kids end up in serious trouble as adults."

"That's what I think, too," Savannah agreed. "I

made so many mistakes when I was young. I wanted to help my children avoid making the same ones. I didn't expect other adults to actively try to sabotage my efforts."

"You can't let them influence you, Savannah. You do what's best for your son and let them worry about theirs."

She nodded, appearing to contemplate his words.

Kit found it rather odd that he was sitting here dispensing parenting advice to the woman he'd been obsessed with for the past two weeks. Until yesterday, he hadn't even known she had children.

He couldn't say for certain that it would have made any difference to him if she had known. He might have given a bit more thought to the ramifications of becoming involved with a single mother, but he suspected that he would still have come looking for her.

A young waitress shuffled up to their table. "What can I get you?"

Without looking at the menu, Savannah ordered a cup of vegetable soup and a turkey sandwich. Figuring she knew the restaurant, Kit ordered the same for himself.

When the waitress ambled away, obviously in no hurry to turn in their order, Savannah sighed, seemed to shake off her family problems—at least temporarily—and looked directly up at Kit.

"I'm sorry," she said. "You couldn't possibly be interested in discussing my son's misadventures."

"Now, that's where you're wrong," he corrected her, brushing a stray strand of hair away from her temple. Even that brief contact made his fingers tingle. "I'm interested in everything about you."

A light wash of pink tinged her cheeks. He had her

attention now, he thought in satisfaction as their eyes met. For just a moment, the intimacy they'd shared on Serendipity returned, and their surroundings seemed to fall away. For just a heartbeat, there was no one in the little diner except Kit and Savannah.

And then, to Kit's disappointment, a clatter of dishes made Savannah blink and look away, breaking the spell.

She cleared her throat. "I've been telling everyone the story you came up with. I think they believe it."

She didn't sound entirely certain of that, but Kit nodded. "I could tell it made you uncomfortable for people to think there was anything personal between us."

"That's because there isn't. We hardly know each other."

He slipped an arm along the back of the booth, so that his fingers were only inches from her shoulder. He scooted just a bit closer to her on the curved vinyl bench, making it impossible for her to ignore their proximity. He knew his tactics were working when the flush on her cheeks darkened.

"You keep saying that, but I don't agree," he murmured. "We got to know each other pretty well on that island."

She shot him a quick look of disbelief. "Hardly. I never told you I have twin teenagers. You never mentioned that you were a well-known writer. We didn't even exchange last names."

He shook his head. "Details," he said. "We got to know each other on a much more fundamental level."

With his free hand, he touched her lower lip, silently illustrating just how fundamental that level had been. He knew the taste of her, he was reminding her. The feel of her. He knew what it was like to have her trembling in his arms.

And he couldn't wait to have her there again, he told her with his eyes.

Though he knew she'd heard every word of his unspoken message, she looked quickly away and tried to speak firmly. "We both like old movies, old music, picnics and dancing," she said, her voice tight. "That just about sums up everything we have in common."

He thought about it a moment, then nodded. "It's a pretty good start."

"For what?" she asked, looking genuinely puzzled.

Kit was exasperated. "What do you think, Savannah? That I've spent all this time thinking about you because I was curious? That I bullied an old friend for your last name and was prepared to call every McBride in Georgia just so I could stop by and say 'hi'? That I came all this way just to have soup and a sandwich with you in some out-of-the-way diner before I head back to L.A.?"

She twisted her fingers on the table in front of her. "I don't see how there can be anything more."

"I think there can be a whole lot more," Kit returned evenly. "We made a pretty special connection on Serendipity. Can you honestly tell me that you didn't feel it, too?"

She couldn't seem to quite meet his eyes. "I—er—"

He leaned closer to her, so that his lips almost touched her ear when he murmured, "Tell me you haven't thought about me at all during the past two weeks, and I'll accept that it was all one-sided. I'll believe that I read something into it that just wasn't there."

"It wasn't all one-sided," she conceded after a momentary hesitation. "I felt something, too. But I convinced myself that it was because of the surroundings. The romantic atmosphere. The unreality of it all."

The slow-moving waitress dropped a tray full of dishes on the other side of the diner. The resulting crash made the few patrons in the place jump, Kit and Savannah included.

"Shit," the young woman said loudly, and bent at the waist to clean up the mess, exposing more backside beneath her short skirt than she probably realized.

Kit couldn't help laughing. And then he grew abruptly serious as he looked down and found Savannah gazing up at him.

"We're hardly in the most romantic surroundings now," he pointed out. "This place is definitely grounded in reality. But it doesn't change the way I feel being with you."

He watched her as she swallowed. He saw the pulse fluttering in the hollow of her throat, and he wanted nothing more than to bury his lips there.

"I don't know what you want me to say," she murmured.

"Just tell me how you feel."

"Flattered," she admitted. "Confused. A little skeptical. Very nervous."

He nodded, intrigued by her choice of words. "Well, that's honest, anyway. What makes you most nervous—me, or my reputation?"

"Your reputation," she answered without hesitation. "I'm perfectly comfortable with Kit, the man I met on the island."

He smiled. "That's exactly what I hoped—"

"But," she broke in firmly, "I'm not at all comfortable with Christopher Pace, the famous writer. You're prime gossip material, and anyone who is seen with you gets caught in the backlash. I don't want to find my photograph in some sleazy tabloid with all the details of my life spread out for any curious grocery shopper to read."

He looked at her thoughtfully. "You've had some experience with the tabloids?"

"I've had all too much experience with gossip," she answered wearily. "And I swore I'd never again put myself in the middle of it."

The waitress approached with a loaded tray. She set their lunches in front of them with only a minimum of soup-sloshing and dish-rattling, then drifted away without asking if they needed anything else.

Kit glanced down at his food, found that he had no appetite, then looked back at Savannah, who seemed no more interested in the meal than he was.

"Do you know why I went to that island alone?"

She shook her head. "I assumed you needed a vacation."

"That's an understatement. I wasn't satisfied with my work, with the direction my career was taking, with the future I saw ahead for me. I couldn't remember the last time I'd felt happy." He reached out to cover her hand with his on the table. "But I was happy when I was with you."

He heard her breath catch in her throat. "Oh, Kit."

"You wanted to know why I came looking for you. That's why."

She bit her lip.

"You're wondering what I want from you now, aren't you?"

She nodded a bit warily.

He could certainly understand that. He wasn't sure,

himself, what he'd expected when he came in search of her.

He looked down at their hands on the table. It seemed so natural to touch her. To be with her. He didn't want to go back to L.A. and try to forget her again. For one thing, he knew he would be no more successful at doing so now than he had been before. Not with so many unresolved emotions between them.

He looked into her eyes again, finding their expression troubled—but, he thought hopefully, receptive.

"If I was an insurance salesman, and you and I had met at a church social, and I asked you out to dinner, maybe a movie—what would you say?" he asked impulsively.

Savannah's eyebrows lifted. "Now, how am I supposed to answer that?"

"Honestly."

She shrugged. "I would probably say yes."

"Why?"

She eyed him uncertainly. "Why?"

"Why would you say yes? Because I would seem like a nice enough guy? One you wouldn't mind getting to know a little better?"

"Well...yes. But—"

He nodded, finally satisfied that the biggest problem standing between them was his celebrity status. So all he had to do was convince her that he was just a regular guy who'd been knocked flat off his feet by a very desirable woman—her.

It wasn't going to be easy. For one thing, he wasn't just a regular guy. The Academy Award sitting on the mantel in his apartment had interfered with that, at least until some other screenwriter became the flavor of the month.

He scooted a few inches away from her, then stuck out his right hand, offering it in a classic handshake. "How do you do, Ms. McBride? I'm Kit Pace. I'd love to sell you some insurance, but how about dinner and a movie first?"

He was delighted when she laughed, though it was little more than a reluctant chuckle.

"You're insane, you know," she murmured.

"Probably." He doubted that he would be here now, otherwise. "But I'm relatively harmless. Will you give me a chance to prove that?"

"I told you, Kit. It's not you I'm worried about. It's everything that goes along with being seen with you."

"You're going to let the gossips dictate your life? Are you really going to give them that much power over you?" He deliberately made his tone challenging.

Savannah lifted her chin. "You don't understand."

"Not entirely," he agreed. "And I'd like you to tell me why you're so skittish about the grapevine. But first I want you to tell me that you'll give us a chance. Introduce me to the real Savannah McBride."

She tilted her head and regarded him consideringly for a long moment. And then she reached out and placed her hand in his. "Hello, Kit Pace. I'm Savannah McBride."

His fingers closed firmly around hers. The challenge had been offered and accepted, he realized.

Now it was up to him to make sure both of them won.

WHEN THEY'D FINISHED eating their cold soup and warm turkey sandwich—she had chosen the diner more for its privacy than the quality of its food—Savannah told Kit that she had to get back to her office. He paid for their meal, then walked her to her car.

"What time shall I pick you up tonight?" he asked.

She started to give him a time, then suddenly slapped a hand against her forehead. "I can't go out with you tonight."

He immediately looked suspicious, and she knew he thought she was running scared again. "Why not?"

"My son has a baseball game. I had to miss his last one because I worked late. I really can't miss again tonight."

He relaxed. "Then I'll go with you to cheer him on."

Savannah almost groaned. She could already hear the talk *that* would cause. But she couldn't think of any way to ask him not to go without being rude, *or* confirming his accusation that she allowed the town gossips to rule her actions.

"It really won't be much fun," she assured him. "It's hot at the park. Crowded. Loud. Dusty."

He nodded, and the corners of his mouth twitched with a smile he seemed to be repressing. "I've been in a few ballparks in my time. I know what to expect."

Kit Pace was a very stubborn man, Savannah realized with an inward sigh of defeat. He wasn't going to back off unless she specifically asked him to go away and forget all about her. And, even though she knew that was exactly what she should do, she couldn't make herself say the words.

Kit's smile widened. He touched her cheek with a gentle finger, his eyes sympathetic. "I'll be good. I promise I won't embarrass you."

"You won't have to," she answered glumly. "Everyone else will make certain of that."

He grew serious. "I wish I could promise there won't

be any gossip, Savannah. But there will be. It's just an unpleasant part of life we have to learn to deal with—particularly *my* life. I don't agree that a person who becomes successful in the entertainment industry should automatically forfeit the right to privacy, but that seems to be the way we operate in this country. I don't like it, but I've learned to live with it."

Savannah told herself that it was only a ball game. Surely the gossips couldn't make too much of that. Especially since Kit had put out the story that he was researching small-town life. What better place to begin than at the ballpark?

She nodded. "I'll see you later, then. Why don't you just meet me at the park at six?"

He nodded, listened carefully to the directions she gave him, then stepped back to allow her to open her car door.

"Savannah," he said as she slid beneath the wheel and prepared to drive away. "Thanks for giving me—giving *us*—a chance. You won't be sorry."

"I hope not, Kit," she murmured, turning her key. "I truly hope not."

"CHRISTOPHER PACE is coming to my ball game? Are you kidding?" Michael's eyes were huge with excitement.

"Cool," Miranda breathed. "Maybe he's going to write a book about futuristic terrorists taking over a Little League game or something."

Michael rolled his eyes. "Oh, yeah, right. I'm sure that's exactly what he'll do."

"It could happen," Miranda answered defensively. "Huh, Mom?"

"I have no idea," Savannah replied. "I don't have a writer's imagination."

"Man, I can't believe he's coming to watch," Michael murmured, hitting his fist into his worn baseball mitt. Michael's baseball record was not stellar, but he loved the game with a passion Savannah had never quite understood.

"Reality check," Miranda taunted. "He isn't coming to watch you. He's coming to check out the atmosphere. And maybe," she added impishly, "to check out Mom. I saw the way he was looking at her last night."

Savannah flushed.

Michael's eyes narrowed speculatively.

"So you guys aren't, like, dating or anything, are you?" he asked his mother, looking as if he couldn't decide whether he approved of that idea or not.

"Of course they're not dating," Ernestine snapped, entering the kitchen just in time to hear her grandson's question. "The man is here on business. Why would a man who dates fashion models and movie actresses be interested in your mother?"

Michael's expression cleared. "Uh, yeah. I guess you're right."

Savannah frowned. "Thanks a lot, both of you."

Michael seemed to realize that his words hadn't gone a long way toward endearing him to his mother. "I didn't mean you aren't pretty or anything. It's just that Christopher Pace goes out with women who are...like, the glamorous type, you know? You...well, you're a *mom*," he explained earnestly.

Savannah was feeling older and dowdier by the moment. "We'd better go," she said, glancing pointedly at her watch. "Don't forget your cap."

"Hold on. I want to get my purse," Miranda said, dropping her empty cola can into the recycling bin with a clatter.

Savannah lifted an eyebrow. "You're going to the game?"

Miranda hated baseball. She had recently declared that she was never going to that "loud, dusty, tacky" ballpark again, not even to cheer for her brother's team.

"Well, yeah," Miranda answered casually, not quite meeting Savannah's eyes. "Michael's playing tonight, and I think we should both be there for moral support, don't you?"

Her brother snorted loudly.

Savannah looked at her mother, feeling resigned to the inevitable. "Would you like to join us, Mother?"

"Not tonight, thank you. I'm rather tired. You won't mind if I miss your game, will you, Michael?"

He shook his head. "That's okay, Grandma. You get some rest. Man, I can't believe Christopher Pace is going to be there. Wait'll the guys hear about this."

Ernestine turned away.

Savannah suspected that Michael had just unwittingly hurt his grandmother's feelings. "Are you sure you won't come with us?" she asked again. "It'll be fun."

"Thank you, dear, but I have some letters to write. You three run along and have a nice time."

Guilt. Ernestine wielded it so very well, Savannah thought ruefully.

If Kit could cause this much uproar in her own family, Savannah mused with an apprehensive shake of her head, how much worse would it be at the ballpark?

SAVANNAH SOON FOUND out exactly how awkward it could be to be seen with a celebrity in Campbellville, Georgia. Everyone at the field seemed to turn and stare when she walked in with Kit, who'd been waiting for her at the gate.

Not that she could blame them, exactly. In his colorful knit pullover and close-fitting jeans, with his luxurious dark hair brushed into a casual, windblown style, he was probably the most gorgeous male who'd ever entered the ten-year-old Joe Don Blankenship Memorial Park.

He was definitely the only Academy-Award winner who'd ever done so.

Savannah hated it that she was suddenly reminded again of the time she'd spent with Vince Hankins. As the local golden boy, he'd always attracted attention whenever he and Savannah were seen about town.

Everyone had watched them, everyone had talked about them—and for a while, everyone had wanted to be like them. And Vince had thrived on the adulation. Until, of course, Savannah had ruined it all. That was the way Vince had seen it. Savannah had screwed up. Not him, of course.

Pushing those old, tired memories out of her mind, she held her chin high and looked for a seat. She heard the whispers as she and Kit and Miranda made their way up the crowded metal bleachers to a bench with enough room for them to sit together. Miranda made sure that Kit sat in the middle, so that she could be seen next to him. She obviously took great pride in showing her friends that she was on easy terms with this famous man.

"Are you really Christopher Pace?" a teenager with

a bad haircut and a worse complexion asked only minutes after they sat down.

Kit nodded. "Yes, I am."

"Cool. So how come you killed off Mick O'Malley in the last book, huh? I really liked him. Couldn't you, like, bring him back to life in the next one or something?"

Savannah thought Kit did an admirable job of appearing to consider the suggestion. And then he shook his head.

"I really can't," he said with just a touch of apology. "There was a body, you know. All his co-workers saw him go down. The guy's dead. But I've got a few new characters in the wings that I hope you'll like as well."

Somewhat appeased, the boy nodded.

Joe Feeney, a thirtyish janitor at the local junior high school, made his way to their seats, blocking their view of the action just getting started on the field.

"I want to talk to you after the game, okay?" he demanded of Kit. "Someplace private. See, I got this idea for a movie. You got the connections, I got the story. It'll be a blockbuster, make us both a fortune."

Kit's friendly smile didn't waver. "Thank you for offering me the opportunity, but I'm already under contract for several more screenplays."

"Hey, man, I'm serious. You do not want to pass this up. Just look over my notes, okay?"

"Thank you, but I'll have to pass. Good luck marketing your idea on your own."

Joe seemed inclined to argue, but someone asked him loudly to move, since he was blocking the view of the game. With a grumble, he ambled away, shaking his head in exasperation that Kit had passed up such a fantastic opportunity.

A woman with too much flesh stuffed into a tank top and stretch shorts slid onto the bench in front of them, her mostly bare back only an inch or so from Kit's knees. She had a great deal of hair that had once been dyed yellow-blond, but now had three inches of darker roots showing. Blue eye shadow, false eyelashes, a heavy dose of rouge, and bright red lipstick completed her look.

"Hi, Savannah," she drawled, looking over her shoulder from beneath her half pound of lashes.

"Hi, Treva." Despite the other woman's characteristic flamboyance, Savannah had grown to like her during the years they'd been watching their sons play on the same team.

Treva turned her eyes to Kit. "Who's your cute friend?"

As if she didn't know.

Trying to emulate Kit's patience with stupid questions, Savannah held onto her smile. "Treva Blacklock, this is Christopher Pace."

Treva held out a hand tipped with two-inch-long artificial nails. They were painted a bright scarlet and had little gold accessories glued to them, making them look so lethal that Savannah couldn't fault Kit for hesitating a moment before gingerly shaking Treva's hand.

"Isn't that your Billy about to step up to bat?" Savannah asked Treva, who looked inclined to crawl right into Kit's lap.

Distracted, Treva turned to face the field. "Come on, Billy. Knock that puppy outta' the park!" she yelled through her cupped hands.

"What did I tell you?" Savannah asked Kit in a whisper. "People around here aren't accustomed to having celebrities among them."

He only smiled. "I'm used to it. Stop fretting."

"I am not—"

The crowd surged to its feet, cheering as Billy slammed the ball out into left field, the first hit of the game. Treva pumped her fist and yelled, "Woof, woof, Billy. Way to go!"

A cluster of teenage girls sitting together at one side of the bleachers began to chant, "Go, Bil-ly, Go, Bil-ly."

Kit laughed and shouted, "Good hit, Billy."

Treva sent him a look of approval over her chubby shoulder.

Savannah almost sighed. How could Kit look so darned comfortable here when it should be obvious to everyone that he was completely out of place?

During the remainder of the game, the attention of the crowd seemed to be almost equally divided between the action on the field and Kit.

A reporter for the local weekly newspaper wanted to interview him. Kit promised to give the man a call the next afternoon for a telephone interview, which seemed to more than satisfy the young journalist who rarely—if ever—had the opportunity to interview nationally known subjects.

A burly man in a faded T-shirt and a cap advertising farming equipment stopped by with his hands full of hot dogs and soft drinks from the concession stand. "Just wanted to tell you that I really like your books," he said to Kit.

"Thank you."

"I was laid up in the hospital after I hurt my leg balin' hay last fall. My wife brought me a couple of your books, even though I ain't much of a reader. They kept me from going crazy with boredom. Now I read every one of yours that comes out."

Kit seemed genuinely touched by the plainspoken man's simple praise. "I'm glad my books gave you some pleasure during your ordeal. That's the reason I write them—to entertain."

"Well, keep 'em coming," the farmer said gruffly. "I'll keep buying 'em."

He moved on before Kit could answer.

"Do you know him?" Kit asked Savannah.

She shook her head.

"I think he's Gary Raper's dad," Miranda piped up.

"Find out for me, will you?" Kit requested of her. "I'll send him a copy of my new hardcover."

Miranda nodded, looking pleased with the assignment she'd been given.

A few youngsters shyly approached with pens and scraps of paper for Kit to sign. He signed them all, though he instructed the kids to kneel in the aisle while he did so to keep them from blocking the view of the field from the people surrounding them.

"Mom, I'm thirsty," Miranda said sometime during the fourth inning. "Can I have something from the concession stand?"

"I'll treat," Kit said, beginning to rise.

Savannah placed a hand on his arm. "If you go down there, you'll be mobbed. You won't make it back before the end of the game. Miranda and I will go."

"I'm pretty good at getting through crowds," he said with a cocky grin. "Miranda and I can handle it, can't we?"

Miranda nodded eagerly. "I won't let them mob him, Mom. Let Kit and me go, okay?"

Savannah conceded with a don't-blame-me-if-it's-a-mistake shrug.

"What would you like?" Kit asked her.

"Just a cola," she replied. "Diet."

He nodded and followed an eager Miranda down the bleacher steps.

"Oh, wow, Savannah. He is *so* cute," Treva gushed. "You're so lucky to have a man like that after you."

"Kit isn't 'after' me," Savannah protested. "He's just a friend."

"Yeah, right." Treva snorted inelegantly. "Try telling that to someone who don't have eyes. I seen the way he's been looking at you. Like he'd like to just eat you up or something."

Savannah's face flamed. "Honestly, Treva."

The other woman only laughed. "Hey, don't mind me. I'm only teasing. But, if I was you, I'd give it some thought. The guy's rich and gorgeous. Hang on to him as long as it lasts. And if *you* ain't interested," she added impishly, "have him give *me* a call."

8

TRUE TO HIS WORD, Kit wasn't gone very long. He returned with his hands full of snacks—hot dogs, popcorn, candy bars. A rather smug-looking Miranda tagged close behind him carrying a tray that held four drink cups.

"Are you sure you don't want something to eat?" Kit asked as he took his seat next to Savannah. "Everything smelled so good I got carried away."

She couldn't help smiling as she looked at his haul. "I'd say so."

"So, c'mon, have a hot dog," he said enticingly, waving one in front of her.

Savannah hesitated only a moment before reaching for it. "You talked me into it."

"If only it was always so easy to tempt you," he murmured, his smile wicked.

She looked hastily away from that devastating grin, all too aware of spying eyes. "I don't suppose you remembered the mustard."

He promptly dug into his pocket and pulled out a small plastic packet. "Of course. We couldn't possibly eat hot dogs without mustard."

He made sure their hands brushed when he handed her the condiment. She tried to hide the shiver of response that went through her at the contact.

"So when is Michael going to play?" Kit asked after eating his hot dog in only a few hungry bites.

Overhearing the question, Miranda hooted. "Michael's, like, the worst player on the team," she confided. "He sits on the bench until the team gets way ahead and then the coach sends him in."

"What's his weakness?" Kit asked, frowning.

"Batting. And catching. Probably pitching, too, but he's never been given a shot at that," Miranda answered before Savannah could jump in. "He's been on a team every summer for the past four years—since he was nine—and he never gets any better."

Kit shook his head. "Haven't his coaches worked with him?"

"He's had the same coach all along," Savannah explained. "George Bettencourt—the pitcher's dad," she added.

"We must be ahead," Miranda mumbled around a mouthful of chocolate-and-peanut candy bar. "There goes Michael out to right field."

Savannah automatically tensed. She wanted very badly for Michael to do well today, particularly with Kit watching. She knew how embarrassed her son would be if he played poorly.

But the only hit that went in Michael's direction sailed right over his head. And the only time he got up to bat he struck out.

"Oh, well," Miranda said matter-of-factly. "At least we're far enough ahead that he didn't blow the game."

"The boy can't judge the distance of the ball," Kit, who'd been watching intently, said with a shake of his head. "Have you had his eyes tested?"

"Yes. The optometrist said there was nothing wrong with his eyes."

"Maybe you should have him tested again. By an ophthalmologist, perhaps. Passing a simple eye-chart test doesn't always reveal all visual problems."

"Oh, you're an expert on vision problems, are you?"

Kit grinned and batted his ridiculously long, dark eyelashes. "You think my big, brown eyes are naturally this shiny? Contacts. Astigmatism. *And* I played baseball in high school and college, even considered going pro. I know the game. I can give the boy some pointers, help him compensate a little for his trouble judging distance."

Of *course* he'd played baseball. He'd probably been spectacular at it. The local sports hero, Savannah couldn't help thinking. Just like Vince had been.

But she was doing it again. Comparing Kit to Vince. She had to stop that.

"And if it turns out that my son is just a really bad baseball player?" she asked, trying to keep her mind on their conversation.

He shrugged. "We all have our talents. I'm sure Michael has plenty. But I'll still give him some tips."

Savannah looked at him nervously. She wasn't at all sure that she wanted Kit giving baseball advice to her son—or parenting advice to her, for that matter. She didn't want him getting too deeply involved in her life, when she knew that it was inevitable that he would soon return to his own.

Miranda groaned loudly when a broad-shouldered, shaggy-haired boy swaggered up to the plate. "That's Nick Whitley," she told Kit. "The total creepazoid. He's been bragging all day about how his dad told off Officer Henshaw."

Kit glanced at Savannah. "The one you were telling me about?"

Savannah nodded grimly. "That's the one," she said, noticing Nick's father, who was standing in the stands loudly jeering at the other team's pitcher.

Nick swung and missed.

His father yelled at him. "Watch what you're doing, you numbskull."

Kit scowled. "Nice way to talk to his kid," he muttered.

"It's the way he talks to everyone," Treva said over her shoulder, overhearing Kit's comment. "Guy's a jerk."

Nick connected with the second pitch. He recklessly threw the bat and dashed toward first base. An error on the part of the center fielder sent the ball spinning into the outfield. While the players scrambled to retrieve it, Nick kept running. The crowd cheered him on.

The ball hit the catcher's mitt a half a second before Nick's foot touched home plate. The umpire called him out.

Nick's father came out of the stands, swearing and gesturing, while Nick shouted abuse at the umpire, yelling that he'd been safe and that the umpire was a "stupid, blind old man."

Savannah groaned and resisted an impulse to hide her face in her hands.

How were they supposed to teach these children good sportsmanship—not to mention basic courtesy—when parents behaved this way?

She felt Kit's arm slide around her waist. And, while it felt wonderful—warm, supportive, encouraging—she was quite sure that everyone in the park had noticed his action and would be speculating about just what was going on between Savannah McBride and Christopher Pace.

MIRANDA CAJOLED Kit into following them home for ice cream after the game. Ignoring Savannah's ambivalence, Kit cheerfully agreed.

Ernestine had already gone to bed. She must really have been tired, Savannah thought, hoping Ernestine wasn't coming down with another respiratory infection. Still, it was rather nice not to have her mother's perceptive eyes on them as she and Kit and the twins gathered around the kitchen table with glasses of soda and bowls of butter-pecan ice cream.

"This is great," Kit said, digging in enthusiastically. "Do you always celebrate your team's victories like this, Michael?"

Michael shrugged. "I guess."

"Kit played baseball in high school and college," Miranda announced, beaming with self-importance. "He was going to be a professional ballplayer, but he decided to be a famous writer instead."

Kit chuckled. "I decided to be a writer because I enjoy telling stories. I wasn't really expecting the fame."

"You're definitely famous," Miranda insisted. "It's so cool that you have movies made out of your books. Like Stephen King and Michael Crichton and...and..." She fumbled for another name.

"Tolstoy," Kit supplied roguishly.

Miranda frowned. "What did he write?"

"*War and Peace,*" Savannah murmured.

"Oh. Was Bruce Willis in that one?"

Savannah swallowed a groan.

Kit grinned. "No. That must have been a different one."

SAVANNAH AND KIT stepped out of her front door and into the summer night. It was still quite warm, with no breeze to stir the sultry air. Crickets chirruped loudly in the darkness, their song interrupted only by the occasional bark of a dog and drone of a car engine.

Savannah closed the front door behind them, then leaned back against it. The amber porch light gave enough illumination for safety, but was not so bright that it made them feel spotlighted. Still, she was glad that none of her neighbors seemed to be out.

Kit paused on the porch and gazed around the quiet neighborhood, then turned to her with a smile, planting his right hand on the door beside her. "Have you noticed that we've spent a lot of time together outside at night?"

She was very much aware of his hand, only inches from her shoulder. He'd leaned close to speak softly, so that he loomed over her, crowding her a bit more closely against the door. He probably didn't intend to intimidate her, she assured herself. He was only standing closely enough so that they could talk softly, without risking being overheard.

"We haven't spent a lot of time together at all," she corrected him.

He lifted his left hand and stroked the side of her face with his fingertips. "Always obsessed with details," he murmured.

He was teasing her. She had to force herself to smile. "I'm an office manager. Details are my life."

He slid his fingers down her cheek and along the line of her jaw, just missing the corner of her mouth. "You're an office manager? I didn't know that."

She swallowed. "I, er, I work for a local construction company. I've been with them for ten years."

"Fascinating." He leaned closer to brush his lips across her forehead.

She closed her eyes, which only made her more aware of his warmth, his nearness, the feel of his fingers on her skin.

"I..." Her voice trailed off. She couldn't remember exactly what it was they'd been talking about.

"How old are you, Savannah?"

"I'm...um...thirty." It had taken her a moment to remember.

He kissed the tip of her nose. "You were very young when you had your children."

Her children. She tried to remind herself that they were just inside the door. That she and Kit weren't technically alone—no matter how badly she might wish they were.

"I was seventeen."

"Still in high school?"

She nodded.

Kit's wandering right hand had found the low scoop neck of her T-shirt. He traced the neckline with his fingertip, just brushing the upper swell of her breasts. She felt her nipples tighten in response.

She opened her eyes. He was studying her face, and she knew that his movements weren't random. He knew exactly what he was doing to her.

As if he'd only been waiting for her to look at him, he lowered his head and smothered her mouth with his before she had a chance to prepare herself. Still aware that they were standing in the light of her front porch, Savannah stiffened a moment, then went limp as his grew more thorough, discretion lost in a flood of pleasure.

She could remain rational—at least partially—when they talked.

But when Kit kissed her...

When he kissed her, she couldn't think of anyone or anything but him.

Her arms went around his neck. Her hands tunneled into his thick, dark hair. Her body pressed eagerly against his. She didn't deliberately decide to respond so hungrily to his kiss; it was as if her body decided for her.

She heard a groan rumble in Kit's chest, felt his arms tighten around her.

He tore his mouth from hers for a gasp of air. "I've been wanting to do this for hours," he muttered, then crushed her lips beneath his again before she could confess that she'd been wanting him to.

Kit's hand slid down her back, dipping in at her waist, stopping at her hip to pull her even more snugly against him. She was left in no doubt that he wanted her. Badly.

Whatever obstacles existed between Savannah and Kit—and a tiny, still grimly logical part of her knew there were probably too many to overcome—there was no doubt that the attraction between them was strong, and volatile. It took only a kiss to ignite an explosion of desire. She didn't understand how or why, but the connection they'd made on that island was stronger than ever.

And she didn't know what on earth she was going to do about it.

The embrace might have gone on forever had a pickup truck not sped past, a heavy thud of bass coming from the deafening radio inside it.

The sound broke through Savannah's passion-induced delirium. She broke off the kiss with a gasp, suddenly aware again that they were standing outside on her front porch where anyone could see them. She could almost feel prying eyes trained upon them from behind the curtains of every house nearby, and even though she told herself she was being paranoid, she still found herself hastily putting an arm's distance between herself and Kit.

"You'd better go," she said, her voice almost unrecognizable.

He nodded. "We'll continue this later," he said. She wasn't sure if the words were meant as a promise or a warning.

Uncharacteristically clumsy, she turned, fumbled for the handle and shoved open her door. With cowardly haste, she hurried inside and closed Kit outside. Even as she did so, she knew that the escape was only temporary.

Kit—and her quandary about what to do with him—would return tomorrow.

WHATEVER KIT SAID during the two hours he spent with Michael the next afternoon, it did wonders for the boy's self-esteem, at least when it came to baseball. Michael entered the house chattering about how Kit had taught him to compensate for his "distance deficiency"—Kit's words, apparently.

Michael wanted to call all his friends and brag to them that Christopher Pace had been giving him baseball pointers. He wasn't at all happy when Savannah reminded him that his grounding included telephone privileges. She worried that he hadn't been taking his punishment very seriously over the weekend. Punishment wasn't effective unless it was uncomfortable enough to make him not want to risk receiving it again.

Michael sulked a bit because of her refusal, but was still pleased enough by his afternoon with Kit to let it go without much argument.

Miranda, who'd spent the past half hour practicing a particularly difficult piano piece, was obviously envious that Michael had had Kit's full attention for so long. She was appeased when Kit asked her to play for him, and then effusively complimented her playing. He even sat down on the piano bench beside her and helped her with the section of the piece that was giving her the most trouble.

It turned out that Kit played the piano beautifully, as he demonstrated for them at the twins' urging. He explained that he'd come from a musical family that had instilled a love of classics and musical theater in him. He'd even considered becoming a songwriter instead of a novelist, he added. Michael and Miranda immediately assured him he'd made the right choice by producing his popular books and movies.

Savannah wasn't surprised that Kit played the piano so well—she was beginning to think there was nothing he couldn't do.

The twins were already convinced.

It concerned Savannah that her children were bonding so quickly with Kit. Her son, especially, was so hungry for male attention. Savannah suspected that one reason Michael was drawn to Nick Whitley was because Nick's father was actively involved in Nick's life.

Savannah didn't approve of the way Ernie Whitley overindulged his son and made excuses for everything the boy did, right or wrong, but she couldn't deny that he was very visible. She couldn't blame Michael for being envious, since he'd never even seen his own father.

Miranda, on the other hand, had obviously concocted a romantic fantasy in her mind about Savannah and Kit, and the hints she dropped were anything but subtle. Savannah was sure that Miranda, too, missed having a father, and wouldn't mind filling the position with someone famous, glamorous and wealthy.

Savannah wished she could think of an easy way to warn her children not to become too attached to Kit, or to weave too many daydreams about him. They were too young to understand that some dreams simply weren't meant to come true.

As for Ernestine—well, she seemed to be going out of her way to avoid Kit. Even when she reluctantly invited him for dinner—her deeply-ingrained Southern manners too strong to overcome—she did so without much enthusiasm. Kit accepted, and tried during the meal to charm Ernestine the way he had the rest of the McBride family. He didn't meet with much success. She was polite, but hardly encouraging.

As interested as Ernestine was in being a social success, Savannah would have thought she would welcome a celebrity into their home, and all the fawning attention that accompanied him. Savannah didn't quite understand her mother's wariness where Kit was concerned, unless Ernestine was simply worried that Savannah would be hurt again by another smooth-talking male. And heaven only knew that Savannah had worried enough about that herself.

Maybe because of Ernestine's coolness, Kit didn't linger long after dinner. Once again, Savannah walked him to his car after he bade everyone good-night.

"Your kids seem to like me, but I think your mother

wants me to disappear into thin air," Kit observed dryly when they were alone outside.

Savannah shook her head. "My kids are crazy about you. My mother...well, she's not always the easiest woman to understand," she admitted.

"Mmm. I've always enjoyed a challenge."

His determined tone worried her. Did he consider *her* just another challenge to overcome? Was he the kind who soon grew bored and moved on once he considered himself a victor? Just a grown-up and more experienced version of Vince?

"Savannah." Kit rested his hands on her shoulders and looked down at her.

She tensed, remembering the way he'd kissed her the night before, the way she'd lost all reason. She couldn't do that again tonight. She was too aware of those imaginary eyes watching them.

But all he said was, "I want to spend some time alone with you. We need to talk."

"About what?" she asked warily.

"Everything," he answered simply. "I want to know everything about you. And maybe there are some things you'd like to know about me."

There were definitely a few things Savannah wanted to know about Kit. She just wasn't at all sure she would have the nerve to ask the questions that kept nagging at the back of her mind.

"Will you have dinner with me tomorrow evening? Just the two of us?"

She moistened her lips. "Yes."

He nodded in satisfaction. He brushed his mouth across hers, then stepped back quickly, as though making an effort to avoid the temptation to linger. "I'll see you tomorrow," he said.

Savannah's heart was pounding when she let herself back into the house. Tomorrow it would be just the two of them. And she wasn't at all sure she would be able to keep up the emotional barriers she'd been trying so hard to build between them.

BY THE TIME Kit picked Savannah up Sunday evening for their date, she was well ready to get away from her family. Much as she loved them, there were times when they got on her nerves. Today had been one of those times.

The twins had been hyper all afternoon. They'd both expressed disappointment and envy that Savannah intended to dine with Kit without their company.

Again, she worried that they were growing too accustomed to having Kit in their lives. She was terribly afraid that they would be hurt when he moved on—as, of course, he would. Like most mothers, Savannah hated it when her children were hurt.

In case Kit had not already figured it out, she would have to spend tonight convincing him that she was a mother first and a single woman second. She couldn't chance indulging in behavior that could have repercussions for her children. It was past time she made that perfectly clear.

Savannah didn't invite Kit in when he rang her doorbell. Instead, she slipped outside and closed the door behind her with a guilty sense of relief.

"You look beautiful," Kit told her, admiring her sleeveless red dress. On impulse, she'd worn the tropical-flower pin he'd given her on her left shoulder.

"Thank you." She didn't bother telling him that he looked fabulous in his black slacks and gray patterned shirt. She figured that was a given. Kit couldn't look bad no matter what he had on.

She didn't even want to think about how good he would look without anything on at all. Not if she wanted to carry on a coherent conversation.

Kit waited until they were both belted into his rented car before asking, "What's wrong, Savannah?"

She tried to keep her expression neutral. "Nothing. Why?"

"You look tense."

"I'm fine."

Though he didn't look convinced by her breezy denial, he let it go.

"Michael and I had a good time yesterday," he said instead, making casual conversation as he guided the car away from her neighborhood.

"Yes, he's been talking about it ever since. Apparently, you made him feel much better about his ball-playing."

"He's not bad, really. He just hasn't had any coaching."

Savannah shrugged. "The coach tends to concentrate on the boys with more natural ability, I suppose. His own son seemed to have been born knowing how to pitch. It doesn't come as easily for Michael."

Vince Hankins hadn't even given his son his athletic ability, Savannah thought with a trace of old bitterness.

But she didn't want to think about the past now. And she didn't want to talk about her family. She looked out the window beside her. "Where are we going?"

"I thought I would surprise you."

Savannah wasn't at all sure she liked the sound of that. She'd been dealing with one surprise after another since Kit had arrived in town. She wasn't sure how many more jolts she could handle.

They drove for almost half an hour without saying much, both pretending to listen to the soft music from the radio while they pursued their own thoughts. When Kit turned onto a county road that led toward Lake Sidney Lanier, Savannah assumed he was taking her to a fishing resort restaurant. Instead, he drove toward a secluded cabin at the end of a winding gravel road. Lights burned in the windows, making the little A-frame look welcoming in the deepening dusk.

"This is where we're having dinner?" she asked, her voice breaking a bit with nerves.

He parked the car and nodded. "If it's all right with you," he assured her. "I have a meal waiting inside for us. It will give us a chance to be alone, without interruptions."

She bit her lower lip. While she liked the idea of not worrying about prying eyes, she wasn't so sure she was ready to be this much alone with Kit.

"Savannah, relax," he said, touching her hand. "I promise, I won't ask for anything more than you want to give. Surely you know by now that you can trust me."

She could have told him that she trusted him implicitly. He'd given her no reason not to.

It was herself she didn't trust tonight.

But she couldn't tell him that. Nodding, she reached for the handle of the car door. She would take the evening as it came, she decided. And she would try very hard to keep her feet on firm, level ground.

9

"IS THIS WHERE you've been staying?" Savannah asked, as Kit led her up the gravel pathway to the cabin's doorstep.

"Since Friday. I stayed in a motel Thursday night, but I didn't care for it. So I called a Realtor Friday morning and she directed me to this place. It's quite nice, really."

Savannah suspected that it was also quite expensive. It looked like one of those places wealthy businessmen used to get away from their high-stress jobs on fishing weekends. Sometimes she forgot that Kit was one of the rich and famous. He acted like such an average guy, she thought wistfully.

She wished selfishly that he really was an insurance salesman. That it would make it so much easier to imagine a future with him.

The cabin was rustically decorated, as Savannah had imagined it would be, but the furnishings had obviously been selected by a professional. Comfortably overstuffed sofas and chairs, colorful throw rugs on the polished wood floor, appealing artwork on the panelled walls. A doorway at the back of the living room probably opened into a kitchen. A wooden staircase on the other side led upward to the single sleeping loft.

Savannah refused to look at those stairs.

A small round table flanked by four bow-back chairs sat at the back of the airy living area, but Savannah saw no evidence that Kit was prepared to serve dinner there. Instead, he led her to the glass doors behind the table.

Stepping outside, he flipped a switch.

And Savannah was instantly reminded that Kit was the most romantic man she'd ever known.

The glass doors had led to a large flagstone patio. Tiny white lights had been strung overhead to illuminate the blooming flower boxes and the wrought-iron patio furniture—a round table, four chairs, a clever little serving cart, a glider-for-two, and a couple of invitingly cushioned chaise longues. From where she stood, Savannah had a breathtaking view of the moon-silvered lake.

Kit quickly lit the candles that flanked the centerpiece of fresh flowers on the table. The flickering candlelight created an even more romantic ambience.

"Oh, Kit," Savannah breathed, immeasurably touched by his gesture. Even if this was something he did all the time for the women he dated, no one had ever done anything this special for her. And she loved it.

He pressed another switch and soft, dreamy, instrumental music began to play from unseen speakers.

And then he turned to Savannah. "Well?"

"It's beautiful. Perfect." She looked at him with an unguarded expression. "Thank you."

He caught her left hand and lifted it to his lips. "You're welcome."

For a long, shimmering moment they stood just that way, surrounded by music and candles and flowers, his lips warm against her skin. Savannah held her breath until her head spun from lack of oxygen—or was it just Kit's touch?

It was with a show of reluctance that he drew back. "I'll go get our dinner. I'll be right back."

She nodded, not quite trusting her voice.

He urged her to take a seat at the table, and then disappeared into the cabin, leaving her to enjoy the beautiful, peaceful setting. He wasn't gone long, returning with a large wicker hamper from which he began to unpack china plates, silverware and crystal, followed by covered silver serving dishes.

"I ordered this from a local restaurant this afternoon," he explained. "It's a cold meal that I was able to keep in the refrigerator. I didn't want to waste any time in the kitchen this evening."

"A cold meal sounds fine to me," she assured him. She often ate a light supper on Sundays, when Ernestine usually prepared large, heavy lunches.

Kit served their meal with a skill that spoke of experience.

"I worked as a waiter once," he explained when she complimented his expertise. "Back when I was a struggling young writer who still hadn't published his first book. I was pretty good at it, too."

Savannah lifted an eyebrow. "Is there anything you do badly?" she asked, her tone rather dry.

His grin turned cocky. "Not that I can think of at the moment."

She shook her head in feigned exasperation. "Must be nice to be so confident."

Kit only laughed and filled her wineglass.

The meal was delicious. They listened to music and talked while they ate.

Savannah insisted on hearing about Kit. He was

finding out more about her all the time, she reminded him. But she still knew little about him, except his profession.

He shrugged with a self-deprecating air that didn't really suit him. "I'm not so interesting," he assured her.

"That's not what the tabloids and talk shows seem to think," she retorted, her tone wry. She didn't follow them herself, but she'd heard plenty about Kit's appearances in them now that people knew she knew him.

"I'm the flavor of the month," he replied prosaically. "When I was new at this business, I believed the hype. I nearly fell into the Hollywood trap of believing my own press. Three years ago—on my thirty-first birthday—my dad had a long, no-holds-barred talk with me and told me I was getting obnoxious, and that I'd better keep in mind what really mattered in life. If not, he said, I was going to be left with nothing when the fame fairy moved on to the next lucky sucker."

Savannah couldn't help chuckling. "The fame fairy?"

"That's what we call it. Here today, gone tomorrow. Sometimes nice and pleasant, other times wicked and uncomfortable. Thanks in part to my dad's advice, I've learned to enjoy the good parts of success and to try to ignore the downside. Like the tabloids."

"Your dad sounds like a very nice man."

"He's great. Both my parents are. They've always encouraged me to go after whatever I wanted, never led me to believe there was anything I couldn't achieve if I worked hard enough at it. But they always stressed that enjoying life and living it with honor and dignity mattered more than money. I try to keep that in mind."

"You like what you do?"

"I love it," he answered simply. "All I ever wanted to do was to create stories. Entertain people. It was as if I had no choice—as if I was born to do this. I wanted my work to be appreciated, of course, but I never expected all this other stuff. The talk shows and tabloids, I mean."

He shook his head in apparent amazement. "I had no idea that the public would decide I was as interesting as my stories. Most of it, of course, comes from having a good publicist. Once my photograph got into that embarrassing 'Fifty Most Beautiful People' article, he took it and ran with it. And I guess I'm pretty good at working the TV shows—I like talking to people and making them laugh. Again, I suspect that the public interest won't last forever, though I hope they continue to enjoy my books and films."

Savannah hadn't known about the "Fifty Most Beautiful People" thing. *She* had always thought Kit was gorgeous, but it was a bit daunting to realize that he was officially recognized for his looks.

She couldn't help wondering again what she was doing with a man like this. A man whose life was so diametrically different from hers.

She still found it hard to believe that, with all that attention and all the women he must surely have available to him, Kit had chosen to follow her to Campbellville, to spend the past few days with Savannah and her family.

"You, er, never married?" she asked, toying with her food.

"No. I came close a few years ago. It was during that early flush of success. I was dating a fashion model and I thought I was incredibly lucky to have gotten her attention. But all she was interested in was the fame and the parties and the attention. I realized then that I wanted a marriage like my parents had—one that would be as strong during the bad times as it was during the good. I wanted to be part of a union that held together when everyone else turned away, when there was nothing else to hold on to but each other."

He looked a bit embarrassed by his outburst. "That's the way I always thought of my parents," he admitted. "They have such a great relationship. I've seen them have some pretty heated battles during the years, but I've always known that nothing could come between them for long. I didn't have that with Kyra—and I knew I never would. That was when we went our separate ways. She pretty much shrugged and moved on to the guy who plays the lead character in the films based on my books. They're still together, for now, but I've been hearing rumors that she's getting restless again."

He made a face and refilled her wineglass. "Enough about me. Tell me more about yourself. Why did your mother name you Savannah?"

Caught off guard, Savannah answered automatically. "My parents honeymooned there. I was conceived there. Mother thought it was appropriate."

"What was your father like?"

"Kind. Funny. Very hardworking. He died when I was ten."

"I'm sorry."

"So am I."

"Tell me what it was like when you were growing up. How you learned to love the old songs and movies."

A bit awkwardly at first, and then with increasing

ease, she talked to him. Savannah had spent many hours with her grandmother after her father's death, and it had been Grandma McBride who'd loved the old standards and had shared her enjoyment of them with Savannah.

Kit seemed to be fascinated by everything Savannah said. Encouraged by his apparent interest, she found herself revealing more than she'd intended about her youth. She told him about the long hours Ernestine had worked in a grocery store in Honoria to pay for her daughter's stylish clothes and dance lessons, cheerleader expenses and pageant dresses. It had been so important to Ernestine for Savannah to be popular. She had deliberately sought the kind of attention for her that Kit's father had warned him about.

"Why was it so important to her?"

"Mother came from the wrong side of the tracks, from a poor, rather dysfunctional family that left her with a lot of emotional scars. She wanted better for me, but she was a bit confused about what constituted a truly happy childhood. She measured it in peer popularity. I've learned that there's a great deal more to it than that. I've tried to pass that advice on to my children."

With Kit's prodding, she went on to describe the years since she and her mother had moved to Campbellville, twin babies in tow. She talked about her job with the construction company, the few close friends she'd made there, the challenges of raising twins. How carefully she'd tried to live a quiet, unremarkable life, giving the local gossips little to say about her.

Kit's expression held an understanding that she found oddly touching. "You have a real thing about gossip, don't you? Did people talk badly about you when you had the twins?"

She nodded. "Honoria, the town where I grew up, is very much like Campbellville. Small, tight-knit, well-informed about the lives of its residents. And, yes, the people there talked about me. Particularly when my boyfriend decided to deny his own responsibility by spreading stories that he wasn't sure he was the twins' father. It wasn't true, but he had money and a prominent position in the town, and enough friends willing to lie for him that my reputation was trashed."

Kit reached across the table to lay a hand on hers. She thought she saw a flash of anger in his eyes, and knew that it was directed at the people who'd hurt her. "You didn't have any friends willing to speak up for you?"

"My cousins did, though they weren't taken very seriously because the McBrides already had a reputation for being wild and irresponsible. A couple of my closest friends tried to defend me. No one believed them."

She shrugged. "To be honest, there was some general satisfaction in seeing me brought down a few pegs," she said matter-of-factly. "I'd been head cheerleader and homecoming queen, and I'd gotten pretty spoiled. Just as you did at first—I believed my own publicity. I thought I was hot stuff. Thought I would always be everyone's sweetheart. There were some who believed I deserved exactly what I got."

Again, his expression was sympathetic. "And maybe a part of you agreed with them."

"No, of course not," she protested, though she couldn't quite meet his eyes.

"So why did you move to Campbellville? Isn't one

small town the same as another when it comes to gossip?"

"My mother had a cousin who owned a store here. He offered her a job that allowed her to support us all until I finished school and went to work myself. We talked about moving to a bigger city, like Atlanta or Macon, but she only had the grocery-store experience and she wasn't sure she could find a job right off. Besides, we thought it would be better for the twins, in the long run, to grow up in a small town with good schools and a low crime rate."

"And how did people here react to your arrival with two babies? Did they pry?"

"Some did," she admitted. "Others didn't say anything to my face, but probably speculated behind my back. The majority of the townspeople, though, have been very kind. It's not as if single motherhood is all that uncommon these days, though it's still not accepted quite as calmly in the deep South as it is in Hollywood."

"Did you ever think of having an abortion? It was legal then. You were little more than a child yourself. It would have been the easiest way out for you."

She didn't resent the question. She knew that Kit was trying very hard to understand her. What made her tick. What motivated her.

What frightened her about him.

"I thought about it," she replied. "And I finally decided that it wasn't an option I could live with. I would have spent the rest of my life wondering if I'd made the right choice. And I have never had one day of regret that I chose to have my babies."

He nodded, as if her answer wasn't at all surprising to him. Maybe he was starting to know her, after all.

she thought, shaken by the strength of the bond that had developed between them in such a short time. It seemed so real, so solid. It was going to hurt all that much worse when it snapped.

Dessert was rich, chocolatey, decadent. Savannah put all thought of worry and calories out of her mind and ate every bite. She noticed that Kit refilled her wineglass several times, but she didn't protest. It was a night for indulgence, she decided.

After all, who knew how many more enchanted evenings she and Kit would have?

THEY FELL SILENT as they finished their dessert, and Savannah began to pay more attention to the music. A song she and Kit had danced to on the island began to play just as finished the last bite.

Kit promptly stood and held out his hand. "Dance with me."

She didn't hesitate. She swayed a bit on her feet when she stood, but Kit promptly steadied her by pulling her into his arms.

"I think I've had too much wine," she confessed. "I rarely drink."

"Just lean on me," he murmured, resting his cheek against her hair. "I'll hold you."

It felt so familiar to dance with him. She matched her steps effortlessly to his, only slightly hampered by the uneven flagstones beneath their feet.

She couldn't remember ever dancing with anyone else. Or wanting to.

She felt Kit's lips brush against her temple. She shivered in reaction.

"I think you're trying to seduce me," she accused him.

His chuckle rumbled in his chest, making it vibrate against her breasts. Even that feeling was seductive.

"Is it working?" he asked, without denying her allegation.

It was working all too well.

"No, not at all," she fibbed, and rested her head on his shoulder.

"Liar." He sounded more amused than offended.

Probably because he had no doubt that she was rapidly turning to putty in his hands, Savannah thought in resignation.

They danced close to the back wall of the cabin. Kit reached out and snapped off the overhead lights, so that their only illumination came from the moon, the stars and the candles.

Savannah slid both arms around his neck, burying her fingers in his hair. His lips brushed her temple, her cheek, then sought her mouth. She tilted her head back to give him better access.

The kiss lasted for an eternity. By the time it ended, Savannah knew her world had changed forever.

Sometime between their first dance on Serendipity Island and this dance in rural Georgia, she had fallen desperately in love with Christopher Pace.

She'd done some really dumb things in her life, a tiny part of her brain acknowledged as she lost herself in Kit's embrace. But falling in love with this man had to be the most monumental mistake she'd ever made.

It couldn't work. They were too different. Too many obstacles stood between them. She was going to be hurt.

At the moment, she couldn't seem to care.

Kit's hand slid slowly down her back, following her curves. He swayed slowly in place, hardly dancing now, just holding her while the music flowed softly around them.

Savannah nuzzled into his throat, enjoying the very faint, spicy scent of his aftershave. She felt well-defined muscles beneath his shirt, and longed to explore them with her fingertips. And her lips.

She wanted him. It had been so very long since she'd felt genuine physical desire that she was surprised by the force of the hunger that swept through her.

Kit made her feel like a different woman. Bold. Daring. Reckless. Things she couldn't usually afford to be. But was there really any reason she couldn't be all of those things...just for tonight?

Kit sought her mouth, found it, claimed it. She parted her lips for him, welcoming the eager thrust of his tongue. Wanting so much more.

She murmured her need into his mouth.

He seemed to understand and he pulled her firmly against him, kissing her until her head spun.

His hand slipped between them to cup her right breast, and his thumb swept across her hardened nipple, causing her to shudder in reaction.

"Savannah." He spoke without pulling away, his voice a hoarse growl against her lips. "I've wanted you for so long."

She drew back a few inches to look up at him. The candlelight from the table behind her highlighted his face, letting her clearly see his hunger, his need. He'd looked like this that night on the island, when she'd been so tempted to make love with him. And now his desire seemed even more intense, more demanding.

He wanted her, she thought almost in wonder. Enough that he'd gone to a great deal of trouble to find her. Enough to come all this way to be with her, and then to stay when he discovered that she wasn't an easy woman to be with. Enough to go to this much effort to give her a perfect, romantic evening.

She had no doubt that if she told him she wasn't ready for this next step, he would back away—as he had once before. He would be disappointed, and he would no doubt make every effort to change her mind—but he wouldn't force her. Wouldn't intimidate her into giving him what he wanted.

This was Kit, not Vince.

That comforting awareness was almost as seductive as his beautiful smile.

Taking a deep breath for courage, she slid her hand down the back of his neck, over his shoulder, and across his chest. Then she unfastened the top button of his shirt. And then the next.

Kit caught his breath sharply when she slid her hands inside the open shirt to stroke his chest.

He was as beautiful as she'd imagined he would be, she discovered in delight. Warm and sleek and strong. His muscles flexed involuntarily beneath her exploring fingertips. His nipples were tight and hard when she brushed her palms over them, causing his stomach to tighten in reaction.

And when she moved closer to him, pressing her abdomen against his, she found that the rest of him was equally hard.

He wanted her. And tonight there were no prying eyes. No questioning looks. Nothing hidden between them.

Just the two of them...and the moon and the stars and the music.

"I hope I'm reading you correctly," Kit muttered, his hands gripping her hips to hold her snugly against him. "Maybe you'd better tell me what you want, just so I don't misinterpret anything."

"I want you," she whispered, tugging his unbuttoned shirt from his waistband. She slid her bare arms beneath it, burrowing into his warmth, his strength.

"Tonight? Now?" He seemed intent on making her spell it out.

She nodded against him. "Yes."

"You're very sure?"

"Kit." She laughed softly and looked up at him. "Do you want me or not?"

He moved against her, leaving little doubt of his answer.

"I've never wanted anyone this much in my entire life," he said, sounding so sincere that a lump formed in her throat.

She managed to speak around it. "We have this time together," she said. "Let's not waste it."

The sound he made was part groan, part jubilant laugh. "I don't intend to waste a minute," he assured her, and lifted her against his chest to crush her mouth beneath his.

Savannah felt Kit tremble when he reached for the zipper at the back of her dress. She was trembling, too.

Her dress parted, exposing her back to the cool night air. A moment later, it pooled around her feet, leaving her wearing only a lacy red bra and tiny, matching panties with her high-heeled black sandals. She felt a blush rise on her cheeks.

This was a man who'd once considered marriage to a professional model, she remembered unwillingly. Savannah didn't have the skinny, willowy figure she saw on fashion runways. Her curves were fuller, more mature. She was a thirty-year-old woman who had borne twins, and wore a few thin, white stretch marks as evidence. She wasn't ashamed of those marks—how could she be when they were physical reminders of the children she loved so very much?—but she was aware of them, particularly now.

Kit looked at her for a long time. "You're so very beautiful," he murmured. "In sunlight, or moonlight, or candlelight—you're exquisite."

That carping little voice of reason inside her reminded her that he was a writer. Pretty words were the tools of his trade. It would be incredibly foolish of her to take him seriously.

Well, tonight she wanted to be foolish.

"Thank you," she said, and stood on tiptoe to kiss him.

Kit shrugged out of his shirt, and tossed it aside. He broke away from her only long enough to pull the puffy cushion from the chaise longue and drop it on the flagstone patio. And then he reached for her again, lowered her carefully to the long, soft cushion and followed her eagerly down.

He kissed her mouth, her chin, her throat. Kissed her breasts through the red lace of her bra until her skin tingled beneath the fabric, aching for his touch. Only then did he release the clasp and toss the skimpy garment aside, exposing her tightened nipples.

And then he lowered his mouth again, at the same time sliding his hand down her stomach and beneath the waistband of her rapidly dampening red panties.

She nearly arched right off the cushion in reaction.

Kit murmured soothingly against her breasts, then moved up to nibble at her mouth. His fingertips slid through the thatch of curls between her thighs and pressed deeper, making her ache for him. She clutched at his shoulders with trembling hands, urging her to him.

He refused to be rushed.

He explored every contour of her face with his lips, while his fingers continued their thorough, intimate investigation.

She was intensely aware of the cool night air on her bare flesh, the heat of Kit's body where it covered hers. She wore only the tiny red panties, but Kit was still wearing his slacks. She wanted to feel more of him.

She reached between them to fumble for his zipper, and her hand brushed against the hard shaft beneath.

Kit groaned. "I'm trying to make this last," he muttered, his voice rough. "I've wanted you for so long."

She tugged again at the fastening of his slacks. "I want to feel you."

He pressed a hard kiss against her mouth, then lifted himself away from her just long enough to strip off the remainder of his clothing.

She couldn't help thinking again of that magazine article he'd told her about as he stood before her wearing nothing but moonlight. As far as Savannah was concerned, Kit was *the* most beautiful man in the world. And for tonight, at least, he was hers.

She held out her arms.

Kit came down to her in a rush, his mouth and hands all over her. He removed her panties and tossed them heedlessly away, neither of them caring where they landed. And then he moved slowly down her body as if he was memorizing every quivering inch of her, until her breath was catching in ragged sobs in her throat, until she begged him incoherently to satisfy the desperate need he'd built in her.

When she thought she could take no more without

shattering into a zillion aching pieces, Kit reached out and fumbled for his slacks. Muttering apologies for his clumsiness, he plunged his hand into one pocket and then the other, finally pulling out a small, square foil packet.

"Don't hate me for this," he said a bit ruefully, then ripped open the package with his teeth. "I thought it best to be prepared...just in case."

How could she hate him for being prepared to protect her? Savannah wanted very badly to believe that she would have thought of protection herself in a moment, particularly given her history of recklessness. She would have called a halt before she took that particular risk again, she assured herself. But she was pleased that Kit had thought of it first.

He leaned over her and his eyes met hers. He brushed a strand of hair away from her perspiration-damp face. "If you don't want this, tell me now," he said.

"I've never wanted anything more," she answered simply. "I have wanted you from the first time I danced with you."

"Savannah." Her name was an exultant exclamation on his lips. And then he brought his mouth down on hers as he claimed her body. She cried out, a muffled sound of shock, delight, and then an almost overwhelming surge of pleasure.

Kit didn't make love to her gently. Savannah didn't want him to be gentle. She was no shy, frightened girl, but a woman, with a woman's needs. Savannah was an active participant in their lovemaking, making it very clear that this was what she wanted. That she knew exactly what she was doing.

And Kit made it equally clear that he enjoyed every minute of it.

They came together in an explosion of pleasure so intense Savannah would have almost sworn the ground shook beneath them. Her throaty cry echoed in the darkness, along with his hoarse moan.

And then he gathered her close, bathing her face in kisses, murmuring endearments, holding her until the tremors slowed, until her heart stopped pounding so hard she thought it would break right through her chest.

When her mind stopped spinning enough for her to form a coherent thought, Savannah couldn't help wondering again if there was anything Christopher Pace did badly.

10

THEY TOOK THEIR TIME recovering. Savannah lay against Kit's shoulder, his arms snugly around her as she gazed up at the stars. The words "I love you" whispered through her mind. But, even if Kit was ready to hear them, she wasn't ready to say them. There were still too many unanswered questions, too many strikes against them.

Kit pressed a kiss against her hair. "Are you okay?"

"Better than okay," she answered dreamily. "I'm floating."

He chuckled. "I know the feeling."

She had only one problem at the moment. "Kit?"

"Mmm?"

"I'm thirsty."

He chuckled. "So am I. Why don't we finish that wine?"

Taking their time, they dressed, stopping frequently for kisses and intimate touches. And then Kit poured the last of the wine into their glasses.

"To a perfect evening," he murmured, touching his glass to hers.

"Perfect," she agreed and lifted the glass to her slightly tender lips.

They sat on the glider with their wine. Kit slipped his left arm around Savannah's shoulders and gently rocked the glider with his foot. She nestled against him, savoring the closeness between them.

"I have to go back to L.A. in the morning," Kit said after several long moments of companionable silence.

Her blissful mood immediately dimmed.

"Do you?" she asked, keeping her tone neutral.

"Yes. I have an important meeting tomorrow afternoon, and several interviews scheduled during the coming week to promote my new book. I don't suppose—?"

"What?"

"Could you come with me?"

She shook her head. "No," she answered gently. "I have to work. And I can't leave the twins again so soon after my last vacation."

"They could come, too. After all, they're out of school. They'd have a great time. I could probably arrange a day at Disneyland."

She was touched that he was willing to include her children, but she shook her head again. "I can't, Kit. I have to work."

He sighed faintly. "I expected you to say that, but I thought it was worth a shot."

Even if she hadn't had to work, Savannah couldn't seriously imagine taking him up on his offer. She didn't belong in L.A. She was a small-town girl through-and-through. She would have nothing in common with Kit's sophisticated friends, nothing to say to the high-powered movers and shakers in Hollywood. Not to mention her dread of being caught in the media spotlight with Kit.

She almost shuddered at the thought of seeing her photograph on a tabloid page beneath a coy headline questioning her relationship with the famous Christopher Pace. Or, even worse, photos of her children.

No way, she thought flatly. This was exactly why she'd kept her feelings for Kit unspoken. She couldn't commit to something that simply couldn't work.

She told herself she would have no regrets. Tonight had been a once-in-a-lifetime evening that was worth all the heartache that would surely come.

"At least I'm giving you notice that I'll be leaving in the morning. I'm not slipping away without saying goodbye." Kit's tone was light, teasing, but she could tell that the memory of her departure from Serendipity still stung.

She almost apologized again. She bit the words back because she knew that under the same circumstances she would probably make the same choice. Leaving Kit had been the practical, logical, *safe* thing to do.

She'd had no idea, of course, that he would follow her.

"I'll be back," Kit said, "as soon as I can."

Savannah bit her lip and looked away.

Kit stiffened. "Savannah?"

"Yes?"

"You *do* want me to come back, don't you?"

Did she want him to come back? Oh, yes, she wanted him to. She wanted him never to leave.

But did she think it was a good idea? That was a question she couldn't answer as easily.

"Damn it, Savannah." For the first time since she'd met him, Kit sounded impatient. "How can you run away from me again? Now, after what just happened between us?"

"I'm not going anywhere," she answered.

"Not physically, maybe. But emotionally...you just slipped away again without saying goodbye."

Savannah sighed and ran a hand through her disheveled hair. "I just need time, Kit. Everything between us has happened so quickly. I wasn't prepared for this."

"And neither was I. But that didn't stop it from happening, did it?"

"It's too fast," she repeated stubbornly.

He exhaled loudly, clearly frustrated. "All right," he said after a moment. "I won't push you. But I'm not giving up on us, Savannah. I couldn't stop thinking about you, even when I didn't know your last name. There's no way I can forget you after what has happened between us tonight."

"I don't want you to forget me," she whispered, turning her head to look at him. "I just want you to give me time."

Time to see how her children would be affected. Time to find out exactly how serious Kit was about this budding affair. Time to search her own heart to determine just how much she was willing to risk to be with Kit.

His face softened in the guttering candlelight. "Take all the time you need," he murmured, brushing a strand of hair away from her face. "You'll find that I can be very patient when something is this important to me."

He could be very persistent, as well. And Savannah suspected uneasily that the combination would be very difficult to resist.

IT WAS VERY LATE when Kit took Savannah home. She knew she'd look haggard at the office the next day, but she didn't want the night to end.

Kit kissed her at her door, making the embrace last for a long time before he finally, reluctantly drew back. "I'll call you."

She nodded. "Good luck with your meetings and...and everything."

His mouth crooked into a wry grin. "Thanks."

She started to open her door, then looked at him uncertainly. "Kit?"

"Yes?"

"You, er, wouldn't say anything about me during those interviews, would you? If anyone asks where you've been the past few days, or who you've been with..."

His smile vanished. "I don't talk about my personal life to the media, Savannah. And I don't expose my friends to unwelcome publicity."

She could tell that she'd offended him. "I'm sorry," she said quickly. "It's just...well, I've never dated a celebrity before," she finished lamely.

"You could really tick me off, you know that?" he said, but there was no real anger in his voice. He managed to smile again. "Just trust me a little, will you?"

"I'm trying," she answered seriously. "This isn't easy for me."

"I know." He touched her cheek, the gesture so tender it brought a lump to her throat.

"Good night, Kit," she whispered.

"Good night, love."

With that, he turned and walked away. Savannah let herself inside the house, then leaned back against the door, her knees still weak from his husky endearment.

Love.

She really wasn't prepared for this.

EVERYONE ELSE was already in the kitchen when Savannah walked in the next morning. Avoiding her mother's worried eyes, Savannah headed straight for the coffeepot.

"Well?" Miranda asked avidly. "How was your date with Kit last night?"

"We had a very nice time," Savannah replied lightly. "He took me dancing."

He'd taken her flying...but, of course, this was no time to get into that.

"You certainly got in late enough," Ernestine commented.

"Checking up on me, Mother?" Savannah glanced her way with a forced smile. "Should I remind you that I've outgrown curfews?"

"I'll sure be glad when *I* can say that," Michael muttered beneath his breath.

Savannah leveled a look at her son. "Yes, well, that's going to be a while yet, so get used to it."

"He took you dancing." Miranda was still young enough to be a die-hard romantic, and get away with it. "That is so cool."

Savannah carried her coffee and bagel to the table as Miranda asked, "Why don't you like Kit, Grandma? I think he's really nice."

"Me, too," Michael seconded loyally. "We had fun playing ball Saturday. Nick was so jealous when he..."

"Nick?" Savannah lifted her head and narrowed her eyes at her son. "How did Nick know you played ball with Kit?"

"I...uh..."

"Michael, did you call Nick after I told you not to?"

She could tell by his expression that he had.

"Why would you do something that you knew I'd forbidden?" she said angrily.

Michael was obviously just as angry with himself—but for his slip of the tongue, not for his insubordination. "I just wanted to tell him about me and Kit," he muttered. "We only talked for a couple of minutes."

"I told you no telephone calls—*no* telephone calls for two weeks. That was your punishment for breaking the law Thursday night, Michael. I've allowed you a great deal of leeway—including playing ball with Kit on Saturday—but I will not be deliberately disobeyed again. Is that clear?"

"Yes'm," Michael mumbled.

"Is that clear, Michael?" she repeated. "Because I can always ground you for a month, if I think it's necessary in order to get you to take me seriously."

Michael's eyes widened. "No, don't do that. I won't disobey you again."

"Good. I'll be at work all day, but Grandma will be here to keep an eye on you. You'll back me up on this, won't you, Mother?"

"To keep him away from that Whitley boy?" Ernestine nodded curtly. "I surely will."

Savannah pushed away from the table. "I have to get ready for work. We'll talk about this more later."

"Is Kit coming over tonight?" Miranda asked hopefully.

"Kit had to go back to L.A. this morning," Savannah replied, rinsing her coffee cup.

Both twins groaned. Ernestine didn't look surprised.

Savannah realized that her mother had never answered Miranda's question about why she didn't like Kit. Savannah would have liked to hear the answer to that. As far as she could tell, Kit had done nothing to warrant Ernestine's displeasure.

"Is he coming back?" Michael asked.

"He said he will. But, remember, kids, Kit is a very busy man. You can't expect him to spend much time in Campbellville."

Ernestine's fork clattered against her plate, but she didn't say anything.

"I have to get ready," Savannah repeated with a quick, harried look at the oven clock. "I'm going to be late."

She left a notably pensive family behind her, all of them lost in their own private thoughts. Savannah suspected that Christopher Pace figured prominently in all of their reveries.

She knew he wouldn't be far from her own thoughts that day.

SAVANNAH WALKED into her office that morning and all conversation stopped. The sudden silence was profound—and revealing. Savannah had obviously been the subject of speculation.

"Good morning," Patty said brightly, her round cheeks a bit flushed. "Did you have a nice weekend?"

"Yes, very nice, thank you." Savannah headed for her own desk, keeping her expression neutral.

"So when are we going to get to meet Christopher Pace? I've never gotten to meet a real Hollywood celebrity before."

"Kit went back to L.A. this morning," Savannah explained. "He had meetings and interviews scheduled for this week."

Patty's face fell. "Oh. I was really hoping to meet him. He'll be back, won't he?"

"Perhaps, though I really can't say when. It depends, I suppose, on how much more research he needs for his book." Savannah kept her voice light, airy, as if it really didn't matter to her whether Kit came back or not.

And if she pulled that off, she had more acting talent than she'd ever given herself credit for, she thought wryly.

Apparently, she wouldn't be winning any theatrical awards. Patty's expression was decidedly skeptical when Savannah glanced back before entering her office.

She fended off questions from her co-workers and impertinent commentary from construction-crew members all morning. Her determined refusal to elaborate on her relationship, or lack of one, with Kit finally seemed to be having an effect. By lunchtime, everyone was caught up in the busy work day.

And then the roses arrived. A dozen of them. Red.

"For you, Savannah," Patty said, sailing into her office with the fragrant arrangement in her arms. "Gee. I wonder who sent them."

Torn between delight with the beautiful blooms and dismay that Kit had made such a blatantly public gesture, Savannah tried to smile in response to Patty's jesting tone. "I assume there's a card?"

"Seems to be one tucked in here. Want me to read it to you?"

Knowing Patty was still teasing, Savannah held onto her smile. "No, thank you. I believe I can handle that part myself."

"*He* sent them, didn't he?" As she set the arrangement on Savannah's desk, Patty touched one velvety bloom almost reverently.

"I haven't read the card yet," Savannah evaded.

"Yes, but you know they're from him."

Savannah was spared having to answer when Patty's phone lines began to ring. Clearly frustrated, Patty returned to her desk. But Savannah knew the questions wouldn't go away as easily.

She opened the florist's card with unsteady fingers.

"Think of me," was all it said. No signature. But, of course, none was required.

Her mouth twisted wryly. Kit must surely know that she'd thought of little else but him since he'd appeared on her doorstep only a few nights ago.

SAVANNAH KNEW from the moment she walked into her kitchen that evening that something had upset Ernestine.

"What's wrong?" she asked, worried that Michael had given his grandmother problems.

Ernestine nodded toward the folded newspaper lying on the kitchen table. "You might want to take a look at that."

Reluctantly, suspecting that she wasn't going to like what she saw, Savannah picked up that afternoon's edition of the small, weekly *Campbellville Courier.*

Someone had taken a photograph of Savannah, Kit, and Miranda all sitting together at the ballpark. They looked like a very cozy group, all of them smiling and relaxed. They looked like a family, Savannah couldn't help thinking.

The copy beneath the photograph explained that "bestselling novelist and Academy-Award-winning screenwriter" Christopher Pace had been in town doing research for his next book. The article added that Pace was spending a great deal of time with the Mc-

Bride family, who had apparently invited him to utilize their town for his research.

"I don't know why you seem so upset," Savannah told her mother, laying the paper back down. "There's nothing of particular interest in that article."

"You like having your picture splashed all over the paper, do you? Having people gawk at you?"

"You, more than anyone, should know exactly how much I dislike that," Savannah replied. "But there's really nothing we can do about it at this point, is there?"

"I don't trust him, Savannah. And if you had the sense God gave a goose, you wouldn't, either. The two of you are as different as night and day. He's going to hurt you. Doesn't he remind you of...?

"Kit is nothing like Vince, Mother," Savannah interrupted sharply.

Ernestine only looked at her. "I didn't have to say the name, did I? You'd already thought of it."

"He isn't like him," Savannah repeated, wanting very badly to convince herself as well as her mother.

It wasn't a particularly pleasant evening. The telephone rang incessantly. Miranda gloated because so many of her friends had seen the photograph of her sitting next to Kit. Michael sulked because Savannah wouldn't allow him to talk to his buddies. And Ernestine simply sat in silence and looked worried.

The final straw was when Miranda called Savannah to the phone.

"I don't know who it is," she said. "Some guy. Could you hurry, Mom? I'm expecting another call."

"You've spent about enough time on the telephone this evening," Savannah replied, and took the receiver. "Hello?"

"Ms. McBride? This is Carl Burger from the *Universal*

News. I was a college roommate of Fred Justice, who's now a reporter for the *Campbellville Courier*."

The *Universal News* was a particularly unsavory tabloid that Savannah had seen while standing in line at the grocery store. "I'm sorry, I have nothing to say to you," she said.

"Just a couple of quick questions, ma'am. I understand you're a close friend of Christopher Pace. Is it true that he's just signed a new, multimillion-dollar deal with a major studio for the film rights to his latest book? I've heard this will make him the highest-paid screenwriter in Hollywood history. Can you confirm that?"

"No, I'm afraid I can't. Goodbye, Mr. Burger."

The man was still talking when Savannah hung up. She immediately snapped on the answering machine.

Kit called at ten, just after the twins had headed upstairs for bed.

"Savannah?" he said through the answering machine speaker. "Hi, it's Kit. Call me when you get in, okay? The number is—"

Savannah lifted the receiver. "I'm here, Kit."

"Oh. Hi. Screening calls?"

"Yes. I didn't particularly want to answer questions about your newest Hollywood deal."

There was a moment of silence on the other end of the line before Kit asked, "Who's been asking you about my new deal?"

"Some guy named Burger. He's a reporter for—"

"The *Universal News*," Kit finished with her. "He's a major pest. How did he find out about you?"

"Apparently, he has a friend on the staff of the *Campbellville Courier*. A friend who seemed to think I would have something of interest to tell."

"Or sell," Kit added grimly. "What did you say to him?"

"Only that I had nothing to say to him."

"I'm sorry, Savannah. I really didn't expect this so soon."

She mulled over his wording for a moment. "But you did expect it eventually."

"Yes. I knew there would be some passing interest in our relationship, particularly now, with this new deal pending. I told you, I'm the flavor of the month. Until someone more entertaining comes along—and that could be tomorrow or next week or next month or whenever—the tabs are going to try to find juicy tidbits to report on me."

"I don't particularly like being a 'juicy tidbit.'"

"I didn't expect you to," he replied wryly. "I was hoping you'd have time to prepare before it happened."

Savannah wasn't sure she would ever have enough time to prepare for that kind of exposure.

"It's okay, love. We'll find a way to deal with this."

She couldn't decide whether to concentrate more on his words or on the endearment. This was the second time he'd called her "love." Was that just something he said to the women in his life—or did he mean it?

"You've had more experience with this sort of thing than I have," she said finally. "What can I expect? Are you famous enough that I'm going to have photographers staking out my house hoping to catch a glimpse of you here?"

"I wouldn't think so," he said slowly, though he didn't sound quite certain enough to please Savannah. "I'm not really a photo celebrity. The bounty-hunter photographers don't shadow me the way they do actors and singers. Right now, they're more interested in the details of my new movie deal. They smell money."

Savannah didn't even want to know how much money was involved in the new deal. Kit's fame was intimidating enough. His fortune might petrify her.

"I can't help worrying about it," she told him. "It's not just my own distaste for publicity. I have to protect my children. Can you understand that?"

"Sweetheart, I've known from the night I arrived in Campbellville and saw you with your kids that they would always come first with you. As far as I'm concerned, that's only something else to admire about you. We won't let them be hurt."

He spoke so confidently, as if it would be easy to make sure Michael and Miranda were protected from any unpleasantness. From disappointment and embarrassment, from heartache and disillusion.

Savannah wished she could believe it was that simple.

Kit seemed to think the subject was settled. "I called to tell you that I should be able to get back there on Friday. Are you free Friday evening?"

Torn between the urgings of her mind and her heart, Savannah fought a brief internal battle before saying, "Yes. I'm free."

"Great. Let's take the family out to dinner. Someplace nice. Your mother, too, of course."

"Trying to soften her up?" Savannah asked dryly.

"Yeah. Think an expensive dinner will help?"

"It couldn't hurt. She usually likes that sort of thing."

"Then we'll give it a shot."

While part of her dreaded the public attention the outing would surely cause, Savannah knew that she had to find out exactly what to expect if she and Kit had a chance of making this unlikely relationship work.

"I miss you, Savannah."

They'd been apart just under twenty-four hours. Hardly enough time for him to miss her. And yet she missed him so badly she ached. It was so much easier when she was with him, when doubts and fears evaporated in the heat of his gleaming dark eyes.

"I'll call you again tomorrow, okay? And let me know if that so-called reporter makes a nuisance of himself. I'll do what I can to get rid of him for you."

"Thank you, but I can take care of myself, Kit."

She thought she heard a very faint sigh.

"I have no doubt about that," he said. "Good night, love."

"Good night."

She hung up slowly, and stood for a long, unmoving moment wondering what in the world she'd gotten herself—and her family—into when she'd placed her hand in Kit's for that first dance.

WHEN THE TELEPHONE rang late Wednesday evening, Savannah snatched it up, expecting it to be Kit. Each time he called, she was certain he would tell her he wouldn't be there Friday after all, that something more important had come up. The children would be so disappointed, she thought. And so, of course, would she.

How could he have become so important to them in such a short time?

She answered the phone in her bedroom, where she wouldn't have to risk her mother overhearing her end of the conversation. "Hello?"

"Is this the glamorous, jet-setting, star-dating Savannah McBride?"

Savannah groaned loudly and flopped to the edge of her bed. "I should have known I'd get a call like this from you."

Her younger cousin Emily laughed. "I'm sorry. I couldn't resist. You've got all of Honoria in a twitter. Are you really dating the rich, famous, gorgeous Christopher Pace?"

"I've been seeing a man I met as Kit," Savannah answered candidly, feeling free for the first time to be completely open. "If I had known when I met him that he was 'the rich, famous, gorgeous Christopher Pace,' I might well have run screaming in the opposite direction."

"What's he like?"

Savannah sighed. "Handsome. Funny. Charming. Romantic. A little spoiled, used to having his own way."

"He sounds fabulous."

"He is."

"So, why the worried tone?"

"Why do you think? Because of who he is, of course."

"The rich, famous, gorgeous Christopher Pace," Emily repeated.

"Exactly."

"And you think—what? That you're not good enough for him?"

"It isn't that," Savannah assured her cousin, who sounded incensed at the very idea. "It's just that we have so little in common. I've lived my whole life in tiny Southern towns. I've spent the past thirteen years quietly working and raising my children. I wouldn't know how to behave at a glitzy Hollywood party, and I don't particularly want to learn."

"You mean you're honestly content to spend the rest of your life in Campbellville? Going to the same job every morning, coming home to the same routine every evening? Never doing anything the least bit exciting or adventurous?"

The restlessness in Emily's voice was something Savannah had never heard before. She couldn't remember if it had been there when they'd been together less than three months ago, after the funeral of Emily's father.

"Emily? Is something wrong?"

"No," her cousin answered just a bit too shortly. "I'm fine. I just don't think you should pass up what could be a wonderful opportunity just because you've hardly ever been out of Georgia. It's not as if small town life has been all that great for either of us."

Emily had probably suffered most from the scandalmongers in Honoria, Savannah mused. Emily's mother—her father's second wife—had run off with the married son of a locally prominent family when Emily was just a toddler. And then, fifteen years ago—less than a month after Savannah, Tara and Emily had whimsically buried their "time capsule"—Emily's adored, older half-brother, Lucas, had left town under suspicion of murder. There had never been enough evidence to formally charge him, but he had been tried and convicted in the beauty shops and living rooms of Honoria. Leaving the way he had, without explanation, had only served to further indict him, as far as the locals were concerned.

Despite Emily's steadfast belief in his innocence, Lucas McBride was remembered in his hometown as a man who'd gotten away with murder.

It had been no big surprise to anyone when Savannah, with her reputation for being reckless and snooty, had turned up pregnant in her senior year of high school, or when half the football team claimed to have nailed her. Few had believed Savannah's insistence that she had only been with one boy, Vince Hankins. He was a Hankins, after all, the son of a church deacon, a member of a long-respected family in Honoria.

Savannah was a McBride.

"You can't blame everyone for the ugly rumors spread by some," Savannah reminded Emily. "On the whole, I like living in a small town. It's a safe place to raise my children, and in a real emergency, I know there are people I can turn to."

Despite their flaws and foibles, Savannah knew small town people. She understood them. She was one of them.

Kit was not.

"Well, I wouldn't mind trying something different for a change," Emily said resolutely. "And, someday, I just might."

They didn't talk much longer. Emily encouraged Savannah to follow her heart where Kit was concerned, and not worry about what the neighbors said. Savannah suggested that Emily follow her own advice and pursue her own happiness.

Without deliberately realizing what she was doing, Savannah found herself standing at her open closet after hanging up her phone. She pulled a shoe-box-sized plastic container from a back corner of the top shelf. And then she sat on the bed again and unsealed the lid, staring pensively inside at the bits of glitter and memorabilia that encapsulated her adolescence. And the letter she hadn't had the courage to open when she and her cousins had dug up the chest.

Something made her turn the envelope over in her hand and pry it open. She winced at the sight of the cutesy, curlicued handwriting, the purple ink, which had faded to a sickly blue. And in arrogantly naive detail, she'd spelled out her view of her future. The fame. The adoring fans. The photographs in every fashion magazine. The leading roles in blockbuster films.

The money.

She tossed the letter aside in disgust. "God, I was such a twit."

That materialistic young Savannah would have been thrilled at the prospect of an affair with "the rich, famous, gorgeous Christopher Pace." She would have found his money as attractive as his beautiful face, his celebrity as seductive as his pirate's smile.

Yet none of those things were what had made the adult Savannah fall in love with him.

She had fallen for a man who liked flowers and moonlight and romantic music. A man who was kind to her children, who played baseball and piano, who made love to her with a generosity and tenderness that she'd only fantasized about before.

She'd never even seen him in that other world, she realized in dismay. He had friends, family, a home, a job—an entire life without her. That Christopher Pace was a stranger to her. How could she know if she would love *him* as much as she loved Kit?

She returned the box to the closet shelf. An old maxim echoed annoyingly in her mind.

Be careful what you wish for—you just might get it.

11

SAVANNAH CAME HOME from work Friday evening to find Kit already there, in her living room, her children competing eagerly for his attention. Ernestine was nowhere to be seen.

The intense pleasure that flooded through Savannah when she saw Kit told her she hadn't been even partially successful in getting her feelings for him under control. And to see him here with her children, waiting to welcome her home...well, that only strengthened the foolish longings she'd been fighting.

"Hi, Mom. Look who's here," Miranda announced exuberantly. A thin gold chain that Savannah didn't remember seeing before glittered on Miranda's flailing wrist.

"Hi, Mom," Michael echoed, looking more content than he had in days as he cradled what looked suspiciously like a new baseball mitt in his hands.

Apparently, Kit had brought gifts.

While she was still dealing with that disturbing realization, Kit smiled broadly, crossed the room in three long strides and planted a firm, enthusiastic kiss right on her mouth. It was all Savannah could do not to grab him and kiss him back.

She'd missed him so badly.

"Hi, Mom," Kip quipped when he drew back.

Savannah's cheeks flamed. She was aware that her

children were staring at her, Michael with uncertainty, Miranda with delight. And she was torn between strangling Kit for embarrassing her in front of her children and dragging him off to a private location where she could kiss him exactly the way she wanted to.

"Mom, look what Kit brought me," Miranda said, rushing up to show off the tiny gold bracelet.

"That's...lovely," Savannah said, determinedly pushing memories of moonlight lovemaking aside. The bracelet really was a pretty little piece, not too big or flashy, just right for a thirteen-year-old girl.

"Check out this glove," Michael said. The instantly recognizable scent of new leather preceded him as he approached to show off his own gift. "Cool, huh?"

"Very nice." Savannah glanced from her son to Kit and back again. "I hope you both thanked Kit for the gifts."

"They thanked me very nicely," Kit assured her. "These kids could give lessons in good manners to a lot of the adults I deal with in L.A."

Both Michael and Miranda looked pleased by the praise.

Savannah noted in approval that both her children were dressed to go out, as she'd instructed them to be when she got home. Miranda had on a black-and-white gingham sundress, and Michael wore a bright, color-block shirt with navy chinos. A pair any mother could be proud of, she thought, admittedly biased.

"Where's Grandma?" she asked. "Is she getting ready for dinner?"

The twins frowned. Kit's smile dimmed.

"She's not here," Michael said. "She went over to Mrs. O'Leary's for dinner."

"She said she'd already made plans with Mrs.

O'Leary and that she knew we wouldn't mind if she didn't go with us," Miranda added.

Ernestine hadn't said a word to Savannah about having other plans for this evening. Apparently, she'd come up with the excuse sometime after Savannah had left for work this morning.

Savannah was growing more frustrated all the time by her mother's steadfast refusal to give Kit a chance. Savannah certainly had her own doubts about the wisdom of this relationship, but she wasn't just rejecting it out of hand, as Ernestine had.

Turning to Kit, Savannah said, "I'm sorry. I thought she would be joining us."

"Don't worry about it," Kit answered with a shrug. "I'll just have to keep working on her."

"Kit brought Grandma a really pretty pin," Miranda piped up. "It even had a diamond in the middle of it."

"I, er, hope she thanked you as nicely as the twins did," Savannah said.

"She was very gracious," Kit said, then added optimistically, "I think I'm getting to her."

Ernestine had always had a weakness for baubles, Savannah thought in resignation. A pretty pin, combined with Kit's winning charm—she imagined that Kit was, indeed, getting to Ernestine, despite Ernestine's concern that Savannah would be hurt and humiliated again.

She managed to smile. "It'll just be the four of us, then. Let me take a few minutes to freshen up and I'll be ready to go. Kit, would you like something to drink while I change?"

"I'll get you something, Kit," Miranda offered eagerly. "We have soda or Kool-Aid. Or orange juice."

Savannah was just about to offer a glass of rarely-served wine as an alternative when Kit asked, "What flavor of Kool-Aid?"

"Raspberry," Miranda replied.

"My favorite," Kit assured her. "I'd love a glass."

Miranda dashed off to get it.

Savannah pointed a finger at Kit. "I'd better not see a red Kool-Aid mustache on you when I get back," she warned teasingly. "I'll send you straight to the bathroom to scrub it off before we go out."

Michael laughed. "I've heard that order enough times."

Kit scuffed a toe on the carpet. "I'll drink it carefully," he promised, his dark eyes glinting with amusement.

"Good."

"Better not spill it on the carpet, either," Michael suggested, joining in the fun. "Mom goes totally ballistic over red Kool-Aid stains on her carpet."

"Maybe I should have asked for orange juice," Kit said, feigning an expression of concern.

Miranda overheard him just as she walked in carrying a tall glass of iced, bright red beverage. "I'll get orange juice for you, if you'd rather have it," she said. "I can always drink this."

Kit promptly reached out to relieve her of the glass. "No, I'd better take this. It sounds too dangerous for a teenager."

Michael laughed smugly at Miranda's puzzled expression.

The teasing and camaraderie continued during dinner at the twins' favorite Italian restaurant. Savannah would have had a lovely time had she not been so aware of all the attention they were getting from the other diners. The stares and whispers, the belated double takes of recognition, the speculation at seeing Kit looking so cozy with Savannah and her children.

Savannah was particularly uncomfortable when she realized that Marie Butler and Lucy Bettencourt were dining together just a few tables away. The town's most avid gossip, and a woman with a grudge. No good could come of the barely veiled attention they were paying to Savannah's table.

Several times during the meal they were interrupted by people wanting Kit's autograph—usually teenagers, but occasionally adults. Savannah couldn't imagine deliberately barging in on a private meal just to ask someone to scribble his name on a dinner napkin. How could Kit be so gracious and polite?

The only time Kit balked was when a woman pulled a disposable camera out of her purse and brashly asked if she could have her photograph taken with him.

"Sorry, but I'm having dinner now," he answered with genial firmness. "I'd rather not."

The woman pouted and tried again to convince him.

"Geesh, lady," Michael said, clearly losing patience. "Can't you see the guy's trying to eat?"

The woman stalked away indignantly.

Savannah didn't bother to correct Michael for his rudeness. There were times, she decided reluctantly, when nothing else would get through.

"Is it always like this for you, Kit?" Miranda asked, looking as though she didn't know whether to envy or pity him.

He shrugged. "Some times are worse than others. When I'm at home in L.A., it's no big deal to see me out at a restaurant. There are a lot of bigger stars there for fans to pester. When I'm on a book tour with a lot of advance publicity, or making an appearance in a small town like Campbellville, where the residents don't see many so-called celebrities, then I get a bit more attention."

Savannah approved of his self-deprecating tone, and the way he downplayed his fame to the twins. But that didn't change the fact that he was, in fact, famous. And she still hadn't reached a point where she could think of him comfortably in that light.

She still had a tendency to separate him into two distinct individuals in her mind. Kit, the man she knew and loved. And Christopher Pace, the near stranger.

But she was painfully aware that their relationship could go no farther until she learned to accept both sides of him.

After ordering dessert, Miranda whispered to her mother that she needed to go to the ladies' room.

"Would you like me to go with you?" Savannah offered.

Miranda rolled her eyes. "*Mother.*"

"Oh, excuse me," Savannah said dryly. Then she turned to Kit. "I thought she knew that women always went in pairs."

Kit chuckled, then asked, "When's your next ball game, Michael?"

"Tomorrow night. Are you coming?" Michael asked, trying to hide his eagerness.

"You bet I will," Kit replied.

"Coach says I've been playing a lot better this week. He spent some one-on-one time with me a couple of afternoons."

Savannah's mouth twisted. Michael's coach had heard about Kit's work with her son. He'd immediately claimed that he had been just about to start working with Michael himself. Whether it had been spurred by piqued pride or celebrity imitation, Michael had loved the special attention.

"That's great, Mike. I look forward to watching you play tomorrow."

The sheer joy that Kit's casual comment brought to Michael's eyes caused Savannah's stomach to clench with renewed concern. She was convinced that Kit would never deliberately wound her children, but she didn't know if he realized how vulnerable they could be. It took so little to win their hearts. And so little to break them.

The thought of her own heart being shattered was painful enough, but she simply couldn't bear the thought of her children being hurt. She had tried so hard to balance her own needs against theirs, worked so diligently to make sure that the children would always come first.

Their desserts arrived and Kit and Michael dug in. Savannah waited for Miranda. She looked toward the ladies' room door and frowned when she saw Marie Butler and Lucy Bettencourt walk out, glance her way, then leave the restaurant.

Miranda was certainly taking a long time, Savannah thought in concern. She was just about to go and check on her when Miranda appeared.

It was immediately apparent that something was wrong. Miranda's eager smile had vanished, replaced by a troubled frown and a distant expression.

"Miranda? Is everything okay?"

"Yeah, sure, Mom." Miranda didn't quite meet her eyes as she picked up her dessert fork. "So, did I miss anything while I was gone?"

"Kit's coming to my ball game tomorrow," Michael announced.

"Great." Miranda tackled her dessert without visible enthusiasm.

Savannah glanced at Kit across the table. He, too, seemed to sense that something was amiss with Miranda. He lifted an eyebrow, as if asking if they should pursue it. Savannah gave a tiny shake of her head. Obviously, Miranda didn't want to talk about it now.

Savannah would wait until they got home. But if Marie and Lucy had said something to upset her child, they would be hearing from her very soon.

KIT TURNED DOWN a group invitation to come in after he drove the McBride family home.

"It's getting late," he said. "I'd better go on back to my cabin."

Savannah thought longingly of the cabin where they'd spent the previous Sunday evening. He must be staying in the same one, she thought, wishing she could go there with him again, but knowing she needed to stay here to find out what was bothering Miranda.

"You kids go on in," she said without reaching for her door handle. "I want to talk to Kit for a minute."

She half expected a teasing comment from Miranda. The fact that Miranda only nodded, said, "Good night, Kit," and climbed out of the car gave Savannah even further reason to be worried.

"What's wrong with Miranda?" Kit asked as soon as the kids had gone into the house. "Have I said something wrong?"

Savannah shook her head, wryly amused that Kit

immediately assumed it was something he'd done. "No. She was fine until she went into the rest room."

Kit frowned in concern. "You think she isn't feeling well?"

"I don't know." Savannah thought again of Marie and Lucy leaving the room just before Miranda emerged. She decided not to mention her suspicions to Kit until she'd had them confirmed.

"You'll let me know if there's anything I can do? Let me write down my cell-phone number so you can reach me at the cabin if you need me."

He reached for a small notebook in the console of the rental car, scrawled some numbers on a page, ripped it out and handed it to Savannah. She put the paper in her purse.

"I'm sure everything will be fine. You know how it is with teenagers and mood swings. One minute they're little angels, the next they're showing fangs and claws." She tried to speak lightly to reassure him, hiding her own concern.

"No, actually I don't know much about teenagers," Kit replied. "Other than being one myself a few years back, I haven't had any experience with them."

"You're very good with them."

"I like your kids," he answered simply.

His words touched her, though she tried not to show him how much. "They like you, too."

"I hope so."

Kit shifted sideways in his seat and reached out to touch Savannah's cheek. "I've missed you."

She caught his hand and pressed it against her face. It was the first time he'd touched her since they'd left for dinner. "I've missed you, too," she admitted.

"That's nice to hear. I'm never sure with you," he

surprised her by saying, his expression rueful. "You make me feel like a nervous kid again sometimes. Asking myself questions... 'Does she like me?' 'Does she think about me when I'm not around?' 'Does she think I'm cute?'"

His smile invited her to laugh with him.

She did. "Yes, I like you. And, yes, I think about you when you're not around. And, yes, I think you're *very* cute."

Chuckling, he slid his hand behind her head and pulled her closer.

"You make me happy, Savannah McBride," he murmured, and then covered her mouth with his before she could reply.

This man knew exactly which buttons to push to turn her into oatmeal, Savannah thought as she slid her arms around his neck and responded to the kiss. Every word, every touch, every smile could have been specifically designed to seduce her. And, oh, did he succeed.

He spent a long time exploring her mouth, tasting, testing, savoring. He ran the tip of his tongue along her lower lip, then slipped it between, teasing her into opening for him. Her tongue met his, and the kiss changed from playful to ravenous.

His hand slid very slowly down her side, then back up again to cup her breast. His thumb circled her nipple, slowly, sensually, reminding her of the way he'd kissed her there when they'd made love. He lowered his head to kiss her chin, and then her throat. And then he tugged down the opening of her scoop-necked top to rub his lips against the top of her breasts, which he cupped in both hands.

Savannah threw back her head and clenched her fingers in his luxurious dark hair, her body beginning to throb with the need for more of him.

"I want you." Kit's voice was gruff. "I want you so badly."

She was only a breath away from ripping his shirt off and taking him right there in the car. It took the last ounce of her willpower to draw back, her breathing heavy, her body quivering with regret.

"I'd better go in," she said finally, her voice hardly recognizable. "I have to check on Miranda."

"I know." He made a visible effort to look understanding.

"Good night, Kit."

"I'll see you tomorrow."

Tomorrow. The word had become somehow important to them. Maybe because each time they parted now, it was with the certainty that they would see each other the next day.

As Savannah walked through her front door, dragging a weary, still unsteady hand through her hair, she wondered how long she would have that reassurance.

ALWAYS THE FIRST in bed, Ernestine was already in her room with the door closed and no light shining beneath it when Savannah passed. She was tempted to tap on the door and have a long heart-to-heart with her mother about Kit, but she decided to wait. She wasn't quite ready for that talk herself.

She stopped by Michael's room next. He was just climbing into bed.

He yawned loudly. "I'd better get some sleep so I can play ball tomorrow. Kit said every athlete needs a good night's sleep the night before a big game."

The obvious adoration in his youthful voice was terrifying to Savannah. She wondered if she should try to warn him not to start expecting too much from Kit just yet. If she could only explain to him that everything between herself and Kit was still so tentative, so uncertain.

But she wasn't quite ready for that talk, either, she found. Especially not while her son looked so happy. She merely nodded and leaned over to kiss his cheek. "Good night, Michael. I love you."

"Love you, too, Mom."

Miranda, too, was already in bed, her head almost hidden by her covers.

"Are you sure nothing's wrong, sweetheart?" Savannah probed gently. "You've been so quiet since dinner."

"Just tired, Mom. Good night."

"I love you, Miranda."

"I love you, too."

Savannah closed herself into her own room and rubbed her temples. It almost felt as though a tornado was going on inside her skull. Her feelings for Kit warred with her concerns about the changes he was making in her family's lives, and the conflict was tearing her apart.

She thought again of her mother's fears. Savannah didn't blame Ernestine for worrying. After all, Ernestine had had to pick up the pieces the last time Savannah had made a mistake. But she told herself again that it would be different this time. For one thing, she was an adult now, capable of taking care of herself when something went wrong.

And she knew all too well that something *could* go wrong between her and Kit. But, unlike her mother, she trusted Kit. She had to believe that he wouldn't hurt her deliberately. That he wasn't using her, as Vince had.

The obstacles between them could well be insurmountable, but she refused to believe that Kit was anything but a good man. An honest man. If he'd just wanted another notch on his bedpost, he would have gone after someone with a lot less baggage. Or he would have disappeared for good after he'd made love with her last weekend.

But, instead, he'd come back. And he'd brought gifts for her family. Taken her children to dinner. And left Savannah at her door rather than pressuring for time alone with her because they'd both been concerned about her daughter.

She hadn't fallen in love with a pretty face, she realized with a faint sense of relief. She'd fallen for a man who happened to be rich and famous along with his other very admirable characteristics.

And maybe—just maybe—there was a chance they could make this thing work.

SAVANNAH KNEW the moment she opened the door to Kit the next afternoon that something was wrong. She could tell by the apologetic look on his face.

"What is it?" she asked apprehensively.

He gave her a fleeting smile, then brushed a kiss across her mouth as he stepped past her into the house. "See? You're getting to know me pretty well."

"Well enough to know when there's something you don't want to tell me." She followed him into the living room, then turned to face him, searching his face for clues.

"I have to go back to L.A."

Her stomach sank. "When?"

"Today. This afternoon. My flight leaves Atlanta in an hour and a half, which just barely gives me time to get there after I tell everyone goodbye."

He wouldn't be there for Michael's game that evening, Savannah thought. Michael would be so disappointed.

She would deal with her own disappointment later.

"It's business," he explained. "A last-minute glitch in the new deal. I tried to talk my agent into handling it without me, but he thinks I need to be there."

"I understand," she assured him. "Go take care of your business, Kit."

"Are the kids here? I want to explain to Michael."

"Michael's already at the ballpark. The coach wanted the players there an hour early."

Kit frowned and nodded. "Be sure and tell him I really wanted to stay. I'd be there if I could."

"I'll tell him."

"Is Miranda here?"

"She's in the kitchen with Mother."

Kit glanced toward the hallway that led to the kitchen. "Is Miranda feeling better?"

"Yes. Whatever was bothering her, she seems to have put it behind her. She's been chattering like a magpie this morning. Moody teenager, remember?"

Taking advantage of their momentary privacy, Kit turned to place a hand behind Savannah's head and pull her to him for a quick, hard kiss. "I don't want to leave you again so soon," he groaned.

"I don't want you to go," she admitted. "But I understand."

"Savannah...come with me. We can be back Monday."

"I can't, Kit."

"No, really. Think about it. We could leave now and..."

"Leave?" Ernestine spoke sharply from the doorway into the living room. Miranda stood behind her. "Where are you going?"

"Kit," Savannah said, "has been called back to L.A. on business. I'm not going anywhere, except to Michael's ball game this evening."

Kit nodded in reluctant resignation.

"Kit," Miranda wailed. "You have to leave?"

"I'll be back," he assured her, "as soon as I can."

Miranda didn't look visibly comforted. "Promise?" she asked, her tone intense enough to make Savannah look at her daughter in concern.

Kit smiled. "I promise, Miranda."

Miranda rushed up to him and threw her arms around his waist. "We'll miss you."

Kit looked surprised for a moment, then warmly returned Miranda's hug. "You won't get rid of me easily," he assured her. "I'll be back. And maybe before the summer vacation is over, your mom will be able to get away from work for a few days to bring you and Michael to visit me in L.A."

Miranda looked up at him with shining, hopeful eyes. "Really? That would be so cool."

"I doubt that your mother is going to take you to L.A., Miranda," Ernestine protested. "That's hardly a fit place for children. Drugs and street gangs, that's all you'll find there."

"But, Grandma..."

"Those things do exist in L.A.," Kit acknowledged with more courtesy than Savannah thought her mother deserved. "But there are just as many places that are family-friendly."

"Disneyland is there, Grandma," Miranda reminded her. "At least, I think it's in L.A.," she added with an uncertain look at Kit.

He smiled and nodded. "It's in Anaheim. Not very far at all from where I live."

"Oh, wow."

Ernestine turned and left the room.

Kit sighed. "Definitely a challenge," he murmured. "I was just going to suggest that she would be welcome to come, too. I have a feeling she would have thrown the invitation back in my face."

"Don't worry about her now," Savannah said. "I'll work on her."

Kit nodded. "I have to go."

She bit her lip and nodded. This was the way it was going to be, she told herself a bit sadly. There would be a lot of goodbyes in her future with Kit, however long that would be. And probably quite a few disappointments. He was a man who was in great demand. A man who had a very busy life more than half a continent away from Campbellville.

It would be a miracle if she saw him once a month.

Could the feelings that had developed between them in such a short time survive long separations?

"Savannah." Kit placed his hands on her shoulders and frowned at her. "Stop it."

"Stop what?" she asked, keeping her expression neutral.

"You're pessimizing again. Don't do that."

She managed a small smile. "'Pessimizing'? Is that a word?"

"If it's not, it should be. It perfectly describes what you're doing to us right now. And I won't have it, is that clear?"

She could tell that he was only partly teasing. "I'll try to optimize, instead," she promised.

He grinned. "I like the sound of that much better."

And then he kissed her.

"I'll call you tonight, if I can," he said when he finally drew away. "Tell Michael..."

"I'll tell him. Now, go, before you miss your plane."

Kit took one last long look at Savannah, sent a quick smile in Miranda's direction, and then let himself out the door. It closed behind him with a thud that echoed in Savannah's heart.

Her eyes focused on that closed door, Miranda leaned against her mother's side, her expression somber.

Savannah wrapped her arm around her daughter's waist. "He'll be back."

"Yeah. Sure he will," Miranda answered, obviously trying to sound positive. "He promised."

Savannah nodded and kissed her daughter's cheek. She saw no need to point out that promises, like hearts, were sometimes broken.

12

THE PLAYERS were already in the dugout when Savannah, Ernestine and Miranda arrived. Miranda hadn't wanted to come since Kit wouldn't be there, but Savannah had talked her into it.

"Michael will be so disappointed that Kit couldn't make it," she'd said. "We should go to cheer him on."

Miranda had reluctantly agreed. Savannah had gotten the feeling that it wasn't just her distaste for baseball that made Miranda want to stay at home, but Miranda wouldn't give her mother any other reason. Savannah had finally let it go.

As soon as he saw them, Michael rushed to the chain-link fence that separated the field from the stands. Several of his teammates—Nick Whitley among them—accompanied him, looking eagerly beyond Michael's family.

"Where's Kit?" Michael demanded. "Is he going to meet you here?"

Savannah wished vainly that she could break the bad news to him in a less public place. "Kit won't be here, Michael," she said quietly, knowing his friends could overhear. "He was called back to L.A. on business. Something about his new movie deal."

Michael's face fell in disappointment. "He said he would be here."

"He wanted to come, Michael. But he had no choice."

Nick Whitley snorted loudly and turned away, muttering something to one of the other boys as they headed back to the dugout. Michael scowled.

"Michael?" Savannah asked in concern. "You do understand, don't you? Kit has a job in L.A. He can't just ignore it when he's needed there, even when he'd rather be here watching you play."

Michael nodded. "Yeah, sure. I know his movie deal is more important than my stupid ball game. I was just hoping he could be here."

"Michael—"

But the boy had already turned and dashed after his teammates.

Savannah turned and looked at her mother. "Don't say it."

Ernestine raised her eyebrows. "I didn't say a word."

She didn't have to, of course. Savannah knew Ernestine was worried that Kit was well on his way to breaking not only Savannah's heart, but the children's, as well.

"Hey, Savannah," Treva shouted out from across several people in the bleachers. "Where's that pretty boyfriend of yours?"

"He had to go back to L.A.," Savannah answered, embarrassed that Treva's question had caused so many eyes to turn their way.

"He'll be back," Miranda added. "He promised."

Savannah reflected wryly that the words "he promised" were rapidly becoming Miranda's mantra. She thought she saw skepticism in several of the faces turned toward her, but told herself she was only being paranoid.

The ballpark was crowded that evening, leaving few seats available in the inadequately sized bleachers. Savannah wondered if so many spectators had shown up because it was an important game, or because there'd been a chance that Christopher Pace would be there. And then she scolded herself again for assuming that everyone was interested in her business.

Still, she had the uncomfortable sensation that many eyes were on her as she climbed the bleacher steps. It was something she was just going to have to get used to if she continued her affair with Kit, she told herself flatly. And then frowned as she recognized the term she'd used to describe their relationship. *Affair.* It sounded so tawdry.

She wondered if that was how everyone else saw it.

Spotting an empty stretch of metal bench, Savannah touched Miranda's arm. "There's a place."

Miranda glanced that way, then quickly back at her mother, her eyes suddenly wide and distressed. "Not there, Mom. Let's find another seat," she whispered urgently.

Surprised, Savannah looked again at the seat in question. Marie Butler and Lucy Bettencourt sat right behind the open space, and were watching Savannah openly. Savannah knew they must be there to watch Lucy's grandson, the team's star pitcher.

"Isn't there someplace else we can sit?" Miranda asked.

Savannah abruptly remembered seeing Lucy and Marie at the restaurant the evening before. She was just about to ask her daughter if the town gossips had said something to her when someone behind her yelled,

"Hey, are you going to stand there blocking the aisle all day?"

"Here's a seat, Savannah," Lucy called out cheerfully, pointing to the bench in front of her. "Hello, Ernestine. Nice evening, isn't it?"

Short of an outright snub, Savannah could think of no way to avoid sitting in front of Lucy and Marie. She nodded in response to their cheery greetings and slid onto the bench after her mother. Miranda hesitated only a moment before sitting beside Savannah, though she kept her eyes firmly trained on the players warming up on the field, ignoring the women behind her.

"Your friend isn't with you today?" Lucy asked as Savannah nodded a greeting. "We saw you at the restaurant last night. You all looked quite cozy."

"Kit has gone back to L.A.," Savannah repeated with forced patience. "He had business to attend to."

Lucy and Marie exchanged meaningful looks.

"I suppose our little Campbellville doesn't have much to offer a man who's used to all those wild Hollywood parties and all," Marie murmured. "Didn't I read somewhere that he once dated Julia Roberts?"

"I wouldn't know," Savannah replied a bit stiffly. "I don't read the gossip rags, myself."

She turned to face the field. She heard Lucy and Marie whispering avidly behind her back, though she couldn't hear what they were saying.

Miranda shot a look of disgust over her shoulder, then leaned toward her mother. "Don't listen to them," she murmured. "They don't even know Kit."

Savannah nodded and forced herself to concentrate on the game that was just starting.

"Hey, Mom, look." Miranda pointed to the outfield. "Isn't that Michael going in at shortstop?"

"Why, yes, it is." Savannah was pleasantly surprised that the coach had allowed Michael to start. Michael must be delighted, she thought proudly.

"I bet Nick's mad," Miranda commented. "He usually starts as shortstop. But Michael said coach is still pretty mad at Nick for acting up so bad at the last game."

Savannah winced and glanced automatically toward Ernie Whitley, who was sitting close to the fence, obviously mouthing his displeasure that his son had been left on the bench.

This wouldn't help Michael's already rocky friendship with Nick, Savannah realized. She didn't know whether to be relieved or concerned.

It was quickly apparent that a few extra lessons and a little personal attention hadn't turned Michael into a star baseball player. The first grounder that came his way went right between his feet. And when he did manage to scramble for it, he overthrew second base by several yards, allowing the opposing player to take an extra base.

Miranda groaned and hid her face in her hands.

Savannah heard Lucy whisper something to Marie about Michael getting "special treatment" because he was a friend of "that Hollywood writer." She wanted very badly to turn around and give Lucy a piece of her mind. For one thing, Lucy's son was the coach. If he was giving Michael special treatment, then Lucy should be criticizing her own son, not Michael.

It was so unfair, Savannah fumed, for anyone to be unpleasant to her children because they didn't approve of her relationship with Kit—whether from jealousy or moral judgment, or whatever the reason. Why should her children have to suffer because of her actions? And wasn't this exactly the reason she'd left Serendipity Island the way she had—to keep her own indiscretions from affecting her family?

And then Michael caught a fly ball for the first out. Michael looked almost as surprised as his teammates to find the ball in his mitt.

Savannah and Miranda and even Ernestine cheered heartily. Savannah resisted sending a smug look over her shoulder. And she couldn't help noticing that Nick Whitley was scowling as he watched from the dugout.

Michael's team won the game by one run. Savannah didn't give her son credit for the win—he'd certainly made his share of errors during the three innings he played—but she was proud of his performance nevertheless. And she could tell from his smile when he looked at her through the wire that he was, too.

She knew he was thinking that he wished Kit could have been there to see him. It was a sentiment Savannah shared.

There was a rush to exit the park by spectators hoping to avoid getting caught in traffic. Savannah, Miranda and Ernestine waited a few minutes until some of the pandemonium had subsided before walking down the bleacher steps toward the field where Michael waited for them. Family and friends of Michael's teammates had also gathered around the gate, congratulating the team on its win, talking brightly among themselves.

Savannah noted that Michael stood to one side of the crowd, surrounded by several other boys, Nick Whitley among them. Looking more closely at her son, Savannah tensed. She could see that her son's adolescent temper was about to blow. She sent mental warnings to Michael not to let the other boys' teasing get to him.

Apparently, his ESP wasn't working that afternoon. Before Savannah could move to intercede, Michael flew at Nick with flailing fists. They tumbled to the dirt, wildly throwing punches while their teammates gathered around to shout encouragement. Ernie Whitley turned from a heated discussion with the coach and ran toward the brawling boys. Savannah groaned and hurried after him, aware that her mother and daughter were right on her heels.

A couple of fathers had jumped in to break up the fray. Michael wasn't cooperating. He continued to yell at Nick, doing his best to break away from the restraining hands. Savannah and Ernie Whitley reached their boys at the same time.

"Michael!" Savannah scolded. "What in the world has gotten into you? You know better than to behave this way."

His hand on Nick's shoulder, Ernie Whitley snorted. "You're the one who's always acting like your boy is too good to hang out with mine. Like mine's going to be a bad influence on him or somethin'. Well, it wasn't my boy who just threw the first punch, and there are plenty of witnesses to that."

"I'm sorry," Savannah said, mortified at the very public scene and painfully aware of all the eyes upon them. "I don't know what got into him."

"Don't apologize to him, Mom," Michael said angrily. "You didn't hear what Nick was saying about you. And his father's been saying it, too."

"I don't care *what* he was saying," Savannah retorted. "There is no excuse for this fighting."

"He called you a tramp!" Michael's infuriated shout carried clearly through the crowd that had gathered around them. Several people gasped.

Savannah looked involuntarily at Ernie, her eyebrows rising. "I—er—"

"Well, she's carrying on with that Hollywood guy and everyone knows what *they're* like, huh, Dad?" Nick said smugly. "Dad said any woman who'd have kids without getting married will probably sleep with anybody. Didn't you, Dad?"

Ernie Whitley looked chagrined that his son had repeated his unkind remarks. "Shut up, Nick," he growled, shaking the boy's shoulder a bit too roughly.

"Well, it's true," Nick said, ignoring his father to glare at Michael. "You've been bragging like you're such hot stuff 'cause your mom's been hanging out with Christopher Pace. You've been acting like he's going to be your dad or something. Well, where is he now, huh? You said he was going to be here, but I don't see him. He got what he wanted and then he went back to those Hollywood babes, just like my dad said he would."

A ripple of murmurs went through the avidly eavesdropping crowd.

Coach Bettencourt stood between the boys, gravely shaking his head. "You boys know the team rules about fighting. Michael, you're going to have to sit out the next game on the bench."

"That's not fair," Miranda said with a gasp, stepping up from behind Savannah, shrugging off her grandmother's restraining hand. "Why would you punish Michael and not Nick? Nick's the one who started the fight."

"Michael threw the first punch," Bettencourt insisted. "He knows fighting is against team rules."

"I bet you wouldn't let someone talk about *your* mother like that," Miranda snapped, throwing a disdainful look at Lucy Bettencourt. "And she's the worst gossip in town. She's been talking about my mother, too, but it isn't true. My mom's the best, and Kit *will* be back. He promised."

Savannah was trying to think of something to say that would effectively put an end to this humiliating debacle when she heard a familiar voice from close behind her.

"Yes, I did promise, didn't I? And it looks like I got back just in time."

Miranda whirled, her face lighting up. "*Kit!*"

Michael dropped his fists, his eyes going wide in his dirt-streaked face. "Kit."

Savannah turned more slowly.

Kit was there, standing only a few feet away from her, his dark hair tousled by the summer breeze, his feet planted firmly on the packed dirt of the ball field, his hands resting on his hips in a true pirate's stance. He didn't look like a man to be trifled with as he glanced from Savannah to Ernie Whitley.

"Is there a problem here?" he asked softly.

THE SPECTATORS fell back, silently clearing a path between Kit and Ernie Whitley.

Whitley glanced around him, then cleared his throat. "The McBride boy jumped mine for no reason at all," he told Kit. "But it's over now."

Kit lifted an eyebrow and looked at Michael. "There's rarely a really good reason for fighting, Michael," he said. "It's such an unimaginative way to settle minor differences."

"That's right," the coach said, nodding in relief and looking impatiently at his watch. "Just what I was telling 'em."

Kit didn't take his eyes from Ernie Whitley's florid face. "I suppose the only incentive for *me* to get involved in a fight would be if someone were to say anything unpleasant about my fiancée or her children. I'm afraid I would take great exception to that. Savannah and her kids are a true asset to this community. If anyone has anything to say to the contrary, I assume he would be willing to say it to her face. Or mine," he added, his voice quietly dangerous.

Fiancée. The word rocked Savannah back on her heels. Was Kit only trying to protect her reputation...or was he as serious as he looked?

She heard the whispers, the murmurs, the speculation, but she kept her eyes trained on Kit's grim face.

Whitley opened and closed his mouth a time or two, then cleared his throat. "I didn't know you two was engaged," he muttered.

Nick stared at Kit in awe, then glanced uncertainly at Michael, his expression torn between resentment and what might have been envy.

"I'd suggest you keep it in mind." Coolly dismissing the other man, Kit turned pointedly toward the coach. "Under the circumstances, I don't think one of the boys should be punished and not the other, do you? Maybe you could let it go with a warning to both of them this time."

"I—uh—" The starstruck coach shuffled his feet. "Yeah, I guess that's what we'll do. Boys...no more fighting, okay?"

Michael nodded, scooped his dusty cap off the ground and settled it firmly on his head. And then he looked at Kit, his eyes shining. "I'm glad you're here, Kit."

Kit reached out to straighten the brim of the boy's

cap. "I promised you I would be here, didn't I? I couldn't leave with that promise on my mind. I'm sorry I missed your game. I got stuck in traffic between the Atlanta airport and here."

He'd gotten all the way to the airport before he'd decided to turn around and come back, Savannah realized. Because he'd made a promise to a thirteen-year-old boy.

How could she *not* love him?

"Congratulations on your engagement, Savannah," Lucy called out, bearing down on them with an obvious hunger for details burning in her eyes. "When's the happy day?"

Savannah looked pleadingly at Kit.

With a skill she could only admire, he managed to usher Savannah and her family through the crowd and out of the park, politely responding to comments and questions without actually answering any of them, avoiding conversational delays without actually being rude.

Savannah hoped he could teach her that skill. She had a feeling she was going to need it in the future.

Reaching the parking lot, Miranda turned eagerly to Kit and took his hand. "Did you just say that to make them shut up about Mom, or did you mean it, Kit?" she whispered, blurting out the question Savannah had been asking herself.

Kit looked over Miranda's head to meet Savannah's eyes. "I never say anything I don't mean," he replied quietly.

Miranda squealed and threw her arms around Kit's waist. He returned the hug warmly.

"That'll show ol' Lucy Bettencourt," Miranda said in satisfaction.

"Miranda, did Lucy say something to upset you last night?" Savannah asked.

Miranda nodded, a frown creasing her forehead. "I heard her talking to Marie Butler in the ladies' room," she admitted. "I was in a stall and they didn't know I was there—at least, I don't think they did."

"What did they say?"

"Mrs. Butler said it probably didn't bother Kit that you had, um, illegitimate children, because people in Hollywood do that sort of thing all the time. And Mrs. Bettencourt said that she bet you two already knew each other when you went away for vacation. She said you probably spent the whole vacation having an affair."

Savannah felt her mouth tighten. She was too angry to respond immediately.

It broke her heart that both of her children had heard allusions to their unfortunate parentage. She had never wanted them to think of themselves as mistakes. She'd tried to convince them that, while ideally she would have been older when she'd had them, she still considered them the best part of her life.

How could other people be so cruel as to hurt them over something that was in no way their fault?

Kit blew a sharp breath out of his nose and muttered a short, pithy word in an undertone that Savannah could only hope the children didn't hear. He made a visible effort to control his temper when he spoke firmly to the children and to Ernestine.

"Okay," he said, "here's the story. You all deserve to hear it. I haven't been doing research on a book, though I suppose I'd better come up with a plot involving a small town, now that the rumor has gotten around. Savannah didn't invite me here to do my research. She had no idea that I was going to show up on your doorstep."

The twins looked at him in curiosity, Ernestine in suspicion. "Then what *are* you doing here?" she demanded.

"I met Savannah on Serendipity Island, and I fell for her," he answered simply. "Hard. And, no," he added with a quick glance at the twins, "we didn't have an affair on the island. We talked and we danced, but that's about it. She left thinking she would never see me again, but I missed her so much that I came looking for her. I wanted a chance to get to know her better."

"You mean you came a courtin'?" Miranda asked, her voice squeaky.

Kit was startled into a laugh. Savannah blushed and wondered where in the world her daughter had picked up *that* phrase.

"Yeah," Kit said, "I guess I came acourtin'. Just like ol' Froggie."

"And now you're getting married." Miranda sighed happily as Savannah gulped. "Cool."

"Your mother hasn't exactly given me an answer yet," Kit murmured, looking apologetically at Savannah.

Savannah still couldn't believe Kit kept talking about marriage. They'd only known each other for only a few days!

He must be crazy. But then, she must be, too. Because she knew that if Kit proposed right now, her answer would be yes.

If, that was, he could convince her that he was asking because he loved her, and not because he'd felt pressured into action.

She glanced at her mother and was startled to see a glint of tears in Ernestine's eyes. "Mother?"

Ernestine looked away. "You'll do what you want, of course."

"Mrs. McBride, what have I done to make you dislike me?" Kit asked, looking directly at her.

She refused to meet his eyes. "Nothing. If you want to take my daughter and grandchildren off to California, I guess that's up to them."

Savannah almost groaned as a light went on in her head. Now she thought she understood at least part of Ernestine's hostility toward Kit. Ernestine knew her daughter very well. She would have taken one look at Savannah and Kit together and known that some powerful emotions were at work between them.

It had been only the four of them for so long, comfortable in their small town routines, all of them secure, if not wealthy, on Savannah's salary. This was Ernestine's home, her family, her life. And Kit threatened that.

Kit must have had some of the same thoughts. His tone was gentle when he spoke, his expression kind.

"I never said anything about taking your family to California—at least not permanently," he reminded her. He gestured around the rapidly emptying parking lot, ignoring the people who stared at them from a distance as they climbed into their cars. "Despite the gossip, this seems like a nice place to raise a family. A writer can work anywhere—in Los Angeles, California, or Campbellville, Georgia."

And then he smiled winningly at Ernestine. "But even if we all chose to move somewhere else, there would always be a place for you," he assured her. "You're an important member of this family. They depend on you. They need you. I can't imagine that they'd ever let anyone take them away from you."

The twins shook their heads in fervent agreement. Savannah smiled and kissed her mother's cheek, knowing that the lines around her mother's stern mouth had been caused by years of work and struggle.

"I love you, Mother," she said to the woman who had always wanted only the best for her daughter and grandchildren.

Ernestine blinked rapidly and muttered something brusque and incomprehensible. She wasn't entirely won over, Savannah thought, but she was getting there.

Kit was very good at this sort of thing.

Kit turned back to the twins. "As for the rest of that garbage you heard, that's all it was. Garbage. Your family business is just that. Your business. No one else's. Your mom doesn't owe apologies or explanations to anyone, and neither do you. Right?"

The twins nodded slowly.

"You're great kids, both of you," he added, his face softening. "Your mother and I haven't talked much about her past, but I know that she is a very special woman. And a wonderful mother. I know she's very proud of you both, and that you must be proud of her. Any man who wouldn't want to be part of this great family would be badly misguided."

"Our father didn't want us," Michael said, his plaintive tone betraying an old hurt. "Grandma said."

"Then it's most definitely his loss," Kit said firmly.

Savannah cleared her throat, feeling that it was time for her to start functioning rationally again—something she hadn't quite been able to do since Kit had said the word "fiancée."

"We really shouldn't continue this discussion in a parking lot," she said. "I think we should go. Mother, would you drive the kids home? Kit and I need to go somewhere to talk in private for a while. We'll see you at home later, okay?"

Ernestine nodded and reached for Savannah's car keys.

The twins looked at Savannah anxiously as she waved them to the car.

"He really likes us, Mom," Miranda said over her shoulder.

"We like him, too," Michael added.

"I'll keep that in mind," Savannah told them dryly.

Apparently, her children were letting her know what they thought her answer should be to Kit's indirect proposal.

But first, Savannah had to hear Kit tell her exactly why he wanted to marry her.

"By the way, Michael," Kit called after the boy. "You and I are going to have a long talk later about when fighting is appropriate and when it's not. And about handling conflict in public places like a gentleman."

Michael looked warily back at Kit. "Are you going to lecture me?"

Kit nodded, his expression suitably stern. "Yes, I am."

Michael beamed happily. "Cool."

Kit chuckled and turned to Savannah. His grin died when he saw her expression. He cleared his throat and shuffled his feet in the dirt, looking a bit like Michael when he was called on the carpet for misbehavior. "Um—I guess I'm in trouble, huh?"

"We need to have a talk," she replied.

KIT DROVE STRAIGHT to the cabin. By unspoken agreement, he and Savannah didn't talk on the way, choosing to listen to the old songs playing from the radio while they contemplated their own thoughts.

Kit ushered her inside and closed the door behind them. He glanced a bit wistfully toward the stairs to the sleeping loft. "I don't suppose you wanted to be alone so we could...er..."

"No," she answered, her tone still dry. "I wanted to be alone so we could talk."

At least, that was what she *thought* they needed to do. What she *wanted* to do with him was irrelevant at the moment.

He put his hands in his pockets and made a production of steeling himself. "Okay," he said. "Shoot."

"Didn't it occur to you that you might talk to me *before* you announced our engagement to my mother and my children and half the residents of Campbellville?"

"I didn't plan to make an announcement," he explained carefully. "It just seemed to pop out. But I meant it, Savannah. I wasn't trying to protect your reputation. I want to marry you."

She moistened her lips and wrapped her arms around her waist. "Kit, I don't need a husband."

His eyebrows dipped into a frown. "Er—"

"I've gotten along perfectly well without one for all this time," she continued determinedly. "I've supported myself, my mother and my children. I've weathered the gossip, and can continue to do so if necessary. I don't need anyone's help or pity."

"Savannah, I—"

She drew a deep breath. "*If* I decide to marry, it will be to a man I am desperately in love with, a man who loves me just as desperately in return. I don't want to be married because he feels pressured by gossip or family or...I don't know, guilt or whatever."

Kit's expression cleared. He took a step closer to her. "I love you, Savannah," he said, his voice clear, firm. "Desperately."

Her heart tripped. "You never said so before."

He took another step. "I shamelessly harassed a longtime friend and probably broke a couple of privacy laws to find you. I risked humiliation and rejection to show up uninvited on your doorstep. I've survived looks from your mother that would have made a less besotted man take to his heels. I've left a multimillion-dollar business deal hanging in limbo for the sake of you and your kids. I've just paid an inflated price for this lakeside cabin because we first made love here. What more would you like me to do to prove my feelings?"

She gulped at the sound of that multimillion-dollar deal. And then something else he'd said sank in.

"You bought the cabin?" she repeated, stunned by the extravagant gesture.

He smiled and nodded. "I've grown rather fond of it."

"Oh, Kit." She drew a deep breath and shook her head, telling herself that it would take more than blatantly romantic gestures to convince her that he'd thought this through.

"But you never said you were considering marriage," she said. "Not that there has really been time for us to get around to that, of course," she added quickly.

"You think tonight was the first time the idea had occurred to me?"

Kit pulled his hand out of his pocket. He held a

small, velvet-covered box in his outstretched palm. "Didn't you wonder," he asked, "why I brought gifts for everyone but you yesterday?"

"Well, no, I wasn't expecting a gift." Her eyes were riveted on that little box.

"Open it," he urged.

A diamond ring lay nestled inside the satin-lined case. It was, without doubt, the single most beautiful piece of jewelry Savannah had ever seen. A flood of emotions swept through her, filling her heart with half-fearful joy and her eyes with hot tears.

Kit laid his hand on her cheek. His voice was tender, husky. "I was going to offer this ring to you here at the cabin this weekend. Outside, at night, with the stars and the moon overhead, 'Star Dust' playing in the background. I planned to go down on one knee and beg you to marry me, even though I knew I was taking a risk because we've known each other such a short time."

She drew a ragged breath. "Oh, Kit."

"Last weekend, you asked me for more time and I promised you had it," he continued a bit gruffly. "You once asked me if there was anything I did badly, and I know now that the answer is yes. I'm not very good at waiting patiently for something that I want. I think I've known from the minute I first laid eyes on you on that Caribbean beach that I wanted to marry you. And now that I know that life will include at least two terrific kids, I'm even more convinced that I will be the luckiest man alive if you say yes."

"Yes," she breathed.

"What was that?"

"Yes," she said a bit more clearly. "I'll marry you.

But, oh, heavens, can you imagine how people will talk?"

"Screw 'em," her dashingly romantic swain said inelegantly. "The tabs will run with this for a day or two. The local tongues will wag. And then the talk will die down. Gossips aren't interested in happy, ordinary married couples, which is exactly what I look forward to being with you. I hope my work continues to draw some attention, but I'm perfectly capable of keeping our private life just that. Private. I've been in the spotlight, and I've enjoyed it occasionally. But now I'm ready to leave the fantasy behind and make a real life with you."

"I love you," she said, in case he hadn't already figured that out.

His pirate's smile flashed. "Desperately?"

"Desperately. And it has nothing to do with your fame or your money or your pretty face. I fell in love with the man who could have been an insurance salesman."

He set the ring box on the coffee table, caught her hands in his and lifted them to his lips, visibly moved by her breathless little speech. "Thank you."

And then he pulled her into his arms and kissed her senseless.

Her shorts fell over the back of a rocking chair. Her T-shirt landed on an end table. She had no idea where her bra and panties went when Kit tossed them impatiently aside.

Savannah was still tugging urgently at Kit's clothing when he pulled her onto the couch.

They made love with more urgency than finesse. Savannah knocked something off the coffee table, and it landed on the floor with a clatter. Kit bumped his head on the wooden sofa arm with enough force to make him curse, and then give a muffled laugh into her mouth. They nearly fell off the narrow cushions and tumbled to the uncarpeted wooden floor.

Savannah wouldn't have changed a moment of it.

"I love you, Savannah McBride," Kit said when he could finally speak again.

"I love you, Kit—or Christopher Pace, or whoever you are," she whispered in return. "I have loved you since our first dance."

She remembered the first song they'd danced to. "That Old Black Magic." And it had been magic, the way she and Kit had met and had known immediately that they were meant to be together.

She intended to make the magic last for a lifetime.

HEART OF TEXAS

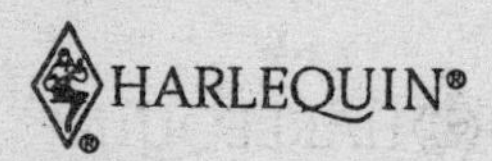
HARLEQUIN®